Logan bent and lifted her but wasn't fully prepared when Grace slid her arms around his neck.

He knew what a come-hither expression looked like and had even experienced it more times than he could count. But he'd never felt the power of it before Grace. He didn't think she even realized how she was looking at him. As if she wanted him, too.

This was big trouble.

It would be so easy to touch his mouth to hers. Only a couple of inches separated them and he ached to know if she tasted of wine, cake and some magic that was all her. Somewhere close by, he heard the chirp of an unlocking car. The sound snapped him out of the sensual trance and he moved over to the truck to set her gently in the passenger seat. It was just a beat too long before she stopped touching him.

"Thanks."

"Buckle up."

He closed the door and realized how stupid he sounded. She wasn't a kid but a grown woman, a fact not lost on him after holding her exceptional curves in his arms.

* * *

THE BACHELORS OF BLACKWATER LAKE:

Dear Reader,

As a parent I struggle with every decision affecting my children. Will I say something profound and life changing or send them into therapy? For this most important job, I'm often flying by the seat of my pants, which means falling back on lessons from my own childhood. It's worked out pretty well so far. But what if one parent was a really bad role model?

Rancher Logan Hunt grew up despising his father because the man cheated on his mother. She finally left with her children because one of his many mistresses was pregnant. There was nowhere to go until her estranged father took them in on the ranch. The experience left deep scars. Marriage and children were not on his list of life goals. Then there was an oops—no marriage because they were better off friends, but he was a father. And so in love with his little girl that his goal changed. It's all about protecting her from himself.

He limits visits to weekends and leaves important parenting decisions to her mother. Then circumstances change and he has sole custody of his five-year-old for two months. With a ranch to run, he hires Grace Flynn, a kindergarten teacher who's off for the summer. Simple, right? But not so much.

Grace was abandoned as a baby and grew up in the foster-care system. All she's ever wanted is a home and roots—somewhere to belong. It was almost hers until love blinded her to a man's manipulation and she has to start from scratch. She's almost there and this summer job will put her over the top again. Nothing will jeopardize that. Including the very strong attraction to her boss.

But love has a mind of its own and Logan's stubborn heart is no match for Grace's sweet determination. She makes him see that sometimes being too careful isn't good for the soul and making a mistake is part of the parental learning curve.

I hope you enjoy reading about these two stubborn people determined to get through a summer with their hearts unscathed. But when love is involved, everything changes for the better. In fact, Grace Flynn is just what the cowboy needed.

Happy reading!

Teresa Southwick

Just What the Cowboy Needed

Teresa Southwick

HARLEQUIN® SPECIAL EDITION®

Recycling programs
for this product may
not exist in your area.

ISBN-13: 978-1-335-46550-4

Just What the Cowboy Needed

Copyright © 2017 by Teresa Southwick

Printed in U.S.A.

Teresa Southwick lives with her husband in Las Vegas, the city that reinvents itself every day. An avid fan of romance novels, she is delighted to be living out her dream of writing for Harlequin.

Visit the Author Profile page at Harlequin.com for more titles.

For everyone who wants a happy ending as much as I do and believes that love will find a way.

Chapter One

Grace Flynn's heart actually skipped a beat, and she'd always thought that happened only in romance novels.

Logan Hunt stood in the doorway of his house, and her worst fears came true. Her first impression was officially correct. He wasn't a troll and that was not good news.

"Hello, Grace. Nice to see you again."

"Nice to see you, too." And that was the absolute truth, darn it.

She'd hoped her attraction to the rancher was an interview thing that would magically disappear on her first day in his employ. Well, she'd just arrived for work and her reaction was even stronger than the last time. Burying her head in the sand wasn't an option. She had to face the fact that she would be living in his house and taking care of his five-year-old daughter for the next eight weeks. This strong response to the man meant the job would be more difficult and complicated than it should be.

On the bright side, and it could just be her stereotyping, men as handsome as this one were usually jerks. The kind who would string a woman along, hint at a future and a family while letting her pour her heart, soul and savings into him and his house, then decide he didn't love her after all. That jerk had used her and stomped on her heart, but being the fool who fell for a pretty face was on her.

"Are you all right, Grace?"

"Yes, fine." She didn't sound breathless, did she? Oh, please no.

Call her pessimistic and cynical, but it wasn't a matter of if Logan would live up to the stereotype, but when. She hoped his inner jerk would come out soon so her heart would stop hammering like a drum at a Fourth of July parade.

"Are you sure?" He was giving her a funny look while standing in the doorway.

Not so much standing as filling it, she thought. He was very tall and boyish looking with his brown hair and blue eyes. Although there was an intensity in those eyes that was all man.

"I'm fine, really. It was a long drive from Buckskin Pass."

"I've been there. Pretty town."

"I like it."

"Please, come in."

"Thanks." She was clutching the handle of her wheeled suitcase and started to roll it inside.

"Let me get that for you."

His fingers touched hers and she felt like a cartoon character whose heart beat so hard and fast you could see the outline of it jumping out of her chest. "Thank you."

"Do you have more in the car?"

"Of course. Packing a lot of stuff is what we do. Women, I mean. I'm a woman."

"Yeah. I noticed." When his gaze met hers, his polite cowboy manner slipped a little. It was the way a man looks at a woman when he likes what he sees, giving her a glimpse of something earthy and primal. And exciting.

That moment of chemistry touched a core of femininity and expectation simmering inside her. Wow. From September to June she was a kindergarten teacher at Buckskin

Pass Elementary School. Without a doubt she could say she had never exchanged a hot look like that with her boss, the principal. But her boss for the summer was a different story.

Grace needed to say something to… What? Break the ice? She was so hot right now, there was no way anything in her immediate perimeter could freeze.

"I'm looking forward to seeing Cassie again. Where is your adorable daughter?"

"She's with her mom doing wedding errands. Tracy will drop her off when they're finished."

"Okay."

Grace had met his ex and liked her a lot. Tracy mentioned that she and Logan had never married, but shared custody of their daughter, although he had her only on weekends. But she was tying the knot and taking an extended honeymoon, so he was keeping their little girl here at the ranch. Since he had to work and needed child care, Grace had been hired to look after her. It would be interesting to know why Logan and Tracy had never married. Why the two of them, who had created a child together and seemed to get along perfectly, hadn't worked out romantically.

"Follow me. I'll show you where you'll be bunking."

The statement was so macho cowboy, she could practically hear the creak of saddle leather and the *clip-clop* of horses' hooves. Or was that just her heart again?

This was the first time she'd seen his house. They'd met in downtown Blackwater Lake at the Grizzly Bear Diner for the interview. So far she liked what she saw. They were standing in the small entryway just inside the front door. There was a living room to the right, dining on the left. Wood furniture looked like well-loved antiques, while the sofa, love seat, chair and ottoman were contemporary, compatible and homey. Somehow it all worked but wasn't what she'd expected from the handsome rancher.

Grace followed him up the stairs. "So, Logan, I checked you out—"

"Oh?" He glanced over his shoulder, but his face gave nothing away.

She couldn't tell whether or not that bothered him. "It's the smart thing to do. I'll be living in your house for eight weeks."

"And looking after my daughter," he reminded her.

"The thing is that you had me checked out, right? I'd expect nothing less from her father."

"Of course I did."

"So it works both ways." Grace was watching for signs that his inner jerk was scratching to be let out. "Can you blame me?"

"Nope." He reached the top of the stairs, then turned right.

"Don't you want to know what I found out?"

He glanced over his shoulder again and appeared amused about something. "As it happens, I know all about me."

Cute, she thought. Actually, he was very cute when he let down his guard a little. She would really like to see what he looked like when he laughed.

"That was more of a conversation starter. Because I found out that this land has been in your family for four generations."

That boggled her mind. He could easily trace his ancestry back to his great-great-grandparents. She, on the other hand, didn't even know who her parents were. That's what happened when shortly after birth you were wrapped in a towel and left at a fire station. Logan had an impressive family tree; she had nothing but question marks.

"I'm aware of that," he finally said.

She was staring at his broad back and wide shoulders and swore it wasn't her imagination that he tensed up. "Happily, nothing bad popped up in the background check I did."

"Good to know."

"And Cassie's mother vouched for you when I interviewed with her."

"What if Tracy was lying?"

"She wasn't."

He stopped in front of a bedroom. "How do you know?"

"I just do."

"You're a good judge of people?"

"Yes." Mostly. Her biggest lapse in judgment was with Lance the Loser.

Everyone was entitled to one monster of a mistake, right? She'd been a kid in the foster care system and had to move from place to place. Growing up, she'd dreamed of having a house of her very own. She'd worked really hard and saved to do that, then lost it on Lance. That's what happened when a girl took a man at his word but got nothing in writing to protect herself.

There'd been no choice but to start all over again saving for a house, and after this summer job, she would have enough for the down payment. Again.

"So, you're a good judge of people and still took this job?" Logan said.

"Is there something you want to tell me?" She was pretty sure he was joking and that was supposed to be a sassy comeback, but Grace couldn't tell if she'd pulled it off.

"You did the research." Logan shrugged and one corner of his mouth quirked up before he carried her suitcase into the spacious room, then set it on a cedar chest at the foot of the bed. "I hope you'll be comfortable here."

There was a queen-size bed with brass head- and footboards. An old-fashioned wedding-ring-patterned spread and throw pillows in dusty rose and green covered the mattress. On the wall over the swivel rocker hung a flowered hatbox and vintage prints in oval frames. One was a needlepoint that said, "A Family Stitched Together with Love Seldom Unravels." The mirrored dresser and matching armoire looked old but well cared for.

"This is a girl's room," Grace observed.

"It was my sister's." He pointed. "The bathroom is through there."

"Lucky girl had it all to herself."

"Not luck so much as practical. Mom and Granddad figured the line would move faster in the morning if Jamie didn't hog the facilities. There's another one down the hall. My two brothers and I used that one. Cassie's room is next to it."

"Wow, four kids." And no mention of his father. "Must have been fun growing up."

"Not really."

It would have been so easy for him to say his childhood was idyllic and carefree. How would she know? Well, except for the glaring omission of any reference to his father. But, really, he could have taken the easy way out and glossed over it, but he didn't. She liked that about him. And yet it made her considerably more curious to know details.

"I'll show you the rest of the place," Logan said, before she could ask anything.

Each room was cozier than the last. The kitchen looked recently remodeled with granite countertops, a large island and wood floor. A circular oak table and four matching chairs filled the nook overlooking a manicured backyard with a pool.

Grace had never had a house of her own and was admittedly sensitive to a homey vibe. That said, after seeing Logan Hunt's whole house there was no denying love at first sight. The realization made the ache inside her bigger. All she'd ever wanted was somewhere to belong with roots that went deep. A place that was all hers, that she could call home.

On the plus side, when this summer job was over she would have the money to put a down payment on property with her name on the title. She could picture it in her mind, a positive affirmation. Until then, her work environment was awesome.

But every plus had a minus, and his name was Logan Hunt.

Logan was doing his damnedest to be a good father, but very often his daughter had a way of proving that he was spitting into the wind.

"Daddy, you got soap in my eyes." Cassie was sitting in the tub, rubbing her eyes.

"Sorry, baby girl." He let the bathwater out, then turned on the tub's spigot and used a plastic glass to pour fresh water over her head. "Is that better?"

She nodded. "I'm cold."

"Got a towel right here." He lifted her out and wrapped the thick terry cloth around her. "Let's get you dry and in your nightgown, then I'll brush your hair."

"I don't like that part." She had blue eyes, light brown hair and the prettiest pout in the world. People always said she looked like him. He would take it, minus the pout part.

"Do you want Grace to brush your hair?"

Cassie thought for a moment. "Maybe you should show her how first."

That meant sharing confined bathroom space with her, but there didn't seem a way out of it. "Okay. I'll go get her while you finish drying off and put on your nightgown."

"Okay."

Logan left and found Grace in her room unpacking. He stood in the open doorway, taking in the fresh pretty sight of her. The first time he'd seen Grace Flynn was when he interviewed her. It felt as if he'd been slugged in the gut with a sledgehammer. The second time was this afternoon when she'd arrived for work, and the sledgehammer felt more like a bulldozer. She wasn't cover-model beautiful, but that mouth… Her full lips looked as soft as cotton candy and twice as sweet. More temptation than he was prepared to deal with.

The problem was, she was perfect for this job, except the part where Logan wanted to find out if she might be attracted to him, too. He would know only if he made a move on her and that was out of the question. But accepting that didn't make the wanting go away. Why couldn't she be a sweet old lady? Or even a crabby one who was great with kids? Since luck had never been on his side, there was no reason to hope for a change now.

Hiring her to take care of his daughter was trouble with a capital *T*, but by the time he'd met her Cassie's mom had all but signed her onto the payroll. His approval was more symbolic than anything, and her credentials were impeccable. No way could he admit he was the problem and why that was. So Grace was here for the next eight weeks.

God help him.

He cleared his throat. "Grace—"

"Oh, my God!" She whirled around, dropping the stack of panties and bras she'd been about to put in a drawer. "I didn't know you were there."

"Sorry. Didn't mean to sneak up on you." It hadn't escaped his notice that her panties were skimpy, lacy and at least one pair was red and one black. Might have been a pink one, too, but verifying would mean staring and that wasn't smart. Sweat beaded on his forehead. "Maybe I should wear a bell around my neck."

"Works for me." She blew out a breath. "Is there something you needed?"

That was a loaded question if he'd ever heard one, but that's not what she meant. "Cassie's finished in the tub and I'm going to brush out her hair. She thought you might want to watch, in case you have to do it."

"Of course. Hair brushing doesn't have a steep learning curve, but she's only five. Easing into the situation to make the transition smoother is a great idea."

"She does have a mind of her own. Sometimes it's better just to go with it." He turned away, knowing she was crossing the room to follow. Not that he was psychic. The scent of her perfume grew stronger and settled inside him. He was pretty sure he could find her in a pitch-black room.

In the bathroom Cassie had pulled some girlie nightgown over her head and stood waiting for them. She grinned. "Hi, Grace. I'm all clean."

"I see that. And your hair is all wet."

"I know. Daddy's going to show you how he combs all the tangles out. He learned from Mommy."

He grabbed the special spray hair product and squirted the liquid on her head, then picked up the wide-toothed comb to slowly drag it from her forehead all the way past her shoulders. "Are you sure you don't want to get all this cut off?"

"No!" Cassie and Grace spoke together.

Logan looked from the small female to the taller one. "I guess it's unanimous."

"Your hair is gorgeous," Grace told the little girl. "Don't let him talk you into cutting it."

"No way." She folded her arms over her chest and glared. "I'm glad Grace is here."

"Yeah." He met her gaze and forced himself not to look at her mouth. If it was up to him, he would advise her to get out before his bad rubbed off on her. Surely there was a woman over sixty in Blackwater Lake who could do this job.

"I'm not going anywhere, sweetie," Grace said. "But I have to say your dad is doing a great job."

"You sound surprised." He continued working out the tangles with the comb.

"Maybe a little. She has thick hair, but you make it look easy."

"Daddy says it's not that different from brushing the horses." Cassie giggled, and her tone said she liked ratting him out.

Humor sparkled in Grace's eyes. "So you use a pricey hair product to detangle horse hair in order to not hurt their delicate scalp?"

"What if I said yes?" He couldn't resist smiling at that.

"I'd say you have some very pampered horses here on the ranch."

On one knee behind his daughter, Logan slowly pulled the plastic comb through the long hair as gently as possible. He wouldn't deliberately hurt her for anything. "Horses are a business asset, and it wouldn't be smart to neglect them. They serve a purpose and need to be maintained. Just like a car or any other piece of equipment."

"Agreed." But she looked puzzled. "And yet, I can't help wondering about the context of the conversation that you had with Cassie, comparing her hair to brushing a horse."

"This little girl wouldn't hold still."

Cassie nodded, throwing off the comb and proving the truth of his words. "Daddy said the horses didn't move while he was brushin' 'em. And he betted me I couldn't be like a horse."

"Did he now?" Grace nodded her approval. "Who won the bet?"

"Daddy did." She sighed. "Holding still is really hard."

"Are the horses older than five?"

"Not all of them." Logan stopped combing and looked up at her. "But I see where you're going with this. Chronological age doesn't work the same in horses as it does in humans."

Cassie had the expression on her face that said she thought he hung the moon. "My daddy knows everything. Don't you, Daddy?"

Logan dreaded the day when she would find out for sure that he didn't know very much of anything. "I know enough to take care of them and keep them healthy. And when it's necessary to consult someone else who knows more than me."

"And you can ride really good, too. Daddy, you promised to teach me how when I was five. And now I am."

His stomach knotted with dread. When he'd promised her that, it had sounded so far in the future. Now, suddenly she was five. Next thing he knew she'd be dating boys and asking to drive a car.

"It's getting late. Why don't we talk about this later, baby girl?"

"That's what you always say." The glare on her face said he was one broken promise away from her realizing that he didn't hang the moon. "And I'm not a baby."

He glanced at Grace and couldn't tell what she was thinking. That pushed him to explain. "It's not just about being five, honey. You have to be strong enough to handle a horse. To show him who's boss."

"And to get strong," Grace interjected, "you have to eat right *and* get enough sleep."

Logan shot her a grateful look for the support and the

distraction that pulled his ass out of the fire. He stood and looked down at his daughter. "That's right."

"Do you like reading a story at bedtime, Cassie?" Grace asked.

The little girl turned serious—and literal. "I don't know how to read yet. But in September I'm going to big-girl school so I can learn."

"How about if I read?" Grace pressed her full lips together, probably to hold back a laugh.

Too bad, Logan thought. He'd heard her laugh and liked it a lot. But he didn't count. Cassie's opinion was the one that mattered and she seemed completely taken with Grace. As comfortable as if she'd known her forever. That was the most important thing. More significant than Grace's pretty sun-streaked brown hair and big hazel eyes.

That did it. No one would ever accuse him of being poetic, so it was a clear sign that the time had come to make himself scarce.

"Okay, baby girl—" He saw the rebellion on the little freckled face and held up his hand. "My bad. You're not a baby. But I'm still going to tuck you into bed, then Grace can read you a story."

"Okay."

Logan took her small hand and they walked to her room. Then he picked her up and set her gently on the mattress before pulling the covers over her. "Sleep tight. I'll see you in the morning."

"Daddy, don't you want to hear the story, too?"

"I'd love to but—" He needed space. "This will give you and Grace a chance to get to know each other. Remember, I won't be around much because I have to work and run the ranch. That's my job."

"So Grace is like Mary Poppins," Cassie said.

"The movie?"

"Yes. Mary Poppins comes to take care of kids and she does magic. When she goes away at the end the whole family is happy."

Logan looked at the woman he'd hired. "I don't know if Grace can do magic, but she's here to watch out for you. Most of the time you'll be with her."

"You still have to teach me to ride a horse, Daddy."

He ignored that and it went into the file of not a hill he was going to die on tonight. Leaning down, he kissed her forehead. "Get some sleep so you grow big and strong."

Logan stood in the hall for a few moments, listening to the sound of Grace's voice reading Cassie's favorite Dr. Seuss book. With a sigh he turned away and headed downstairs, where he was going to try like hell not to think about that woman's sexy underwear on the floor of her room. Or how she might look wearing nothing but those red panties. A good single-malt Scotch might help with that, but liquor traditionally tore down walls and willpower, which was the complete opposite of his current goal.

Coffee was a safer bet, so he poured some that was left over from this morning into a mug and warmed it in the microwave, then headed to his downstairs home office for the inevitable computer work. He wasn't sure how much time had passed when he heard a knock and glanced over to see Grace in the doorway.

"Sorry to interrupt. I just thought you should know that Cassie is asleep."

"Good. Thanks." He started to swivel back to the computer monitor.

"Can I talk to you? About Cassie," she added, as if his distancing himself from her was obvious.

"Of course. Have a seat." The invitation was automatic because he didn't want her to get comfortable enough to stick around.

"Thanks." She sat in one of the club chairs in front of his desk.

"Is there a problem?" He was studying her and saw the color that rose into her cheeks. What was that about?

"No." The response was quick and a little sharp. "Your daughter is wonderful."

"She's the best." And deserved someone without his shortcomings as a father. Unfortunately, he was what she got.

"I just need to know what you expect of me."

He expected that her skin was even softer than it looked, and if he touched his mouth to hers... There it was. His shortcomings as a man were scratching to get out. He shook his head to clear it. "I'm not sure what you mean."

"When I interviewed we talked mostly about my qualifications and obviously my job is to watch over Cassie and keep her safe."

"Did Tracy explain that she thought it best to bring you in before her wedding so Cass can get used to the arrangement? Also, she has a million things to do to get ready for her day. And by the time she leaves on the honeymoon, she'll feel comfortable that everything with our daughter is going smoothly?"

"Yes. She said she'll be gone six weeks."

"Right. So, we're good—"

"Wait. I know you work long hours and won't be around to ask, so it would be good to go over the questions I've thought of, like... How do you want her time structured? Tracy said my application for this job stood out because I teach kindergarten and Cassie will be starting in September. Do you want activities channeled for learning? Or strictly fun?"

Logan had no idea. This was Tracy's deal. She was Cassie's mom and made all the decisions. Since he only ever had his daughter on weekends, Logan deferred to her mother's maternal instincts and judgment. He always had. His upbringing was so screwed up that he had no business deciding anything for his daughter.

He looked at Grace and hoped the panic didn't show. "You're the expert in that department. Do you think she needs learning activities all summer?"

"She's really bright, so probably not. But I can plan some things to do that are fun, and she won't even know she's learning."

"That sounds good."

"For what it's worth, I think kids should be carefree while they can be. Responsibility comes soon enough."

It had come too soon for him. Logan was just a kid himself when his mom took her four children and left his wealthy, cheating father. They ended up homeless, even though she waitressed and cleaned houses, doing her best to take care of them. Logan took on being head of the family to protect her and his siblings. He'd been twelve then and didn't recommend it for any kid.

"Okay," he finally said. "Fun first. No dedicated learning during the summer. Good talk. I'm glad—"

"Wait. Something else I need to ask."

"Shoot." He held in a sigh.

"As far as structuring time... Do you need me to do housekeeping? Cooking? Anything like that?"

"I have someone who comes in once a week, so probably not. But cooking for Cassie and you is something you'll need to handle."

"No problem. I'm happy to plan meals and make a plate for you, if you'd like."

There was a sweetness in her voice, an expression in her eyes, a softness that any man could get used to. And it pierced the hollow emptiness inside him. He was normally dead tired when he finished work at night, and that obviously lowered his resistance. It was his only excuse for saying, "That would be nice."

"Great. Pleased to do it." And she smiled as if that was the truth.

"So, if there's nothing else…"

"Just one more thing."

There always was. "Okay. What is it?"

"Why don't you want to teach Cassie to ride a horse?"

"What makes you think I don't?" He didn't, but that was beside the point.

"I read between the lines," Grace said. "The fact that you always say you'll talk about it later coupled with her protest that she's not a baby. Apparently she feels treated like one."

Logan was pretty sure that at this point in a conversation a mother would fall back on "because I'm the mom and know best." He couldn't do the dad version because he had no idea what the blueprint of a good one looked like. All he could think to say was, "What's your point?"

"Just that I live in a ranching community and teach kindergarten. Lots of children learn to ride even younger than Cassie. So what are you afraid of?"

That he'd be outed as a fraud? The bad that he grew up with was carved into him and would somehow come out and hurt his daughter? "I'm not afraid of anything. But I gave my word to Tracy that our child will be in one cute, adorable piece when she comes back from her honeymoon. You've been hired to help me do that."

"Right." Her tone said she'd noticed he hadn't actually answered her question about teaching Cassie to ride. "That's it, then. Good night, Logan."

He watched the sway of her hips as she left his office, then let out a long breath. Cassie would be fine when this was all over because he'd walk through fire to make sure of it, but he wasn't so sure about himself.

Grace Flynn was unexpected, and nine times out of ten that was not a good thing.

Chapter Two

The next morning after a late breakfast, Cassie wanted to have a tea party outside on the front porch. It was a spectacular late June day and Grace didn't see any reason to say no.

"Let's get our supplies together," she said.

In the spacious family room a very large flat-screen TV was mounted on the wall above the rock fireplace and oak mantel. There was also a very large area in a corner beside it where the little girl's toys were stored. The two of them stood side by side looking at it and taking stock of what they would need.

"Do you want to sit on a blanket and spread out? Or use the outside furniture or your play table? And before you answer, keep in mind that whatever we take outside with us has to be brought back in."

The little girl thought for a moment. "There are only two chairs on the porch, and my table is too little for Daddy. So maybe a blanket, just in case he has time to play there will be enough room for him."

"Does he play with you often?"

"No. Never."

Logan had made it clear that running a ranch took up most of his time and not to expect him to be around much. But there was sadness behind this little girl's resignation and, apparently, a dash of hope that he might one day have a moment to stop and hang with her, if tea party seating to accommodate his size was anything to go by. If they were talking his sex appeal, Grace couldn't imagine a venue spacious enough to contain it. Just an observation, not personal or anything.

"Okay," she said. "A blanket it is."

An old quilt was neatly folded among the games and toys. Grace grabbed it along with a mesh bag full of pink cups, saucers, a teapot and plastic utensils. She took the string handles, then slipped them over her arm. "We'll need this."

"And people, too. But who can I bring?" Cassie tapped her lip thoughtfully. "Ariel has a time-out."

Grace pressed her lips together to hold back her amusement. This child sounded like a miniature adult, and it was so adorable. When she could talk without laughing she asked, "What did Ariel do to get in trouble?"

"She talked back to her mom. And being tired and crabby is no excuse. Moms get tired and crabby, too. But Daddy never does." She picked up another doll and shook her head. "Ella can't go either. Her mom said she had to eat her vegetables and she gave them to the dog."

Grace knelt down and scooped up a soft, pink terry-cloth baby. "How about this cutie?"

"No." Cassie shook her head. "She was whining and her mommy ran out of patience."

Grace noticed that this child was projecting her own experiences on the dolls, and the discipline was clearly mom-centered. "Do their dads ever give them a time-out?"

"No. The dads just smile and pat their heads." There was a wistful quality in her voice, then she brightened. "I know who to bring. Abigail and Hattie. They've been very good and kept their rooms neat and went to bed without complaining."

"Okay, then." Grace watched the child grab two dolls around the neck because her arms were too little to carry both with dignity. "Can you handle those by yourself, kiddo?"

"Yes," she answered proudly.

"I think we might need a blueberry muffin to go along with our tea." Grace had made a batch the previous evening and noticed that Logan ate more than one before he left the house just shy of dawn this morning.

Cassie met her gaze, eyes solemn and hopeful. "That's a good idea. But it might spoil my appetite for lunch."

"Hmm." She didn't want to break rules, but maybe there was wiggle room. "Lunch isn't for a while yet, and if you and I share just one muffin with Abigail and Hattie, that would probably be okay."

The little girl grinned. "You're right. Goody!"

"It's unanimous, then."

Cassie frowned. "What does that mean?"

"It means that you and I agree," Grace explained, then looked at the dolls the child was hanging on to. "Although we should ask Abigail and Hattie whether or not they would like some muffin with their tea."

Cassie looked from one to the other doll. "They both said yes. It's 'nanimous."

Imagination with a dollop of rule breaking was a beautiful thing, Grace thought, knowing that was the kindergarten teacher in her talking. She went into the kitchen and took one of the blueberry muffins out of the leftover container, then joined the little girl on the grass. Together they spread out the blanket, propped up the dolls and arranged plastic plates and utensils in front of all tea party participants.

In the distance you could see the lake and the mountains beyond. The view took her breath away. The barn and corral were at the bottom of the rise, and she could see several horses prancing and playing. Then she sat cross-legged with her back to the sight. At her interview, Logan had mentioned he raised cattle and was doing a little horse breeding, too.

She hadn't seen him since last night in his study and didn't have a clue when their paths would cross again, although his daughter was insistent about having room for him should he show up for the tea party. Grace's heart skipped at the thought and she did her best to ignore the involuntary reaction. Anyway, it was silly. Cassie had told her he never showed up to play.

"Can you cut up the muffin?" Cassie asked. "Abigail and Hattie are gettin' hungry."

"My apologies, ladies," she said to the dolls, and Cassie giggled. "Kiddo, if you would pour tea for our guests, I will take care of the snacks."

Grace didn't know whether or not the plastic play knives had been washed, so she decided to break up the muffin with her hands, as evenly as possible.

"Here you go, Abigail. And some for you, Hattie," she said, placing a bite in front of the blonde and brunette dolls.

"Thank you." Cassie used a high-pitched, pretend voice, obviously channeling either Abigail or Hattie. Then she wolfed down her share of the treat.

Grace's mouth was full when she heard footsteps. The hairs on her neck stood up, and there was a hitch in her breathing. It wasn't necessary to see him to know Logan was behind her, and if there was a God in heaven, she would not choke on her blueberry muffin.

Then he moved into view and spoke in the wonderful, deep voice that turned her insides to mush. "What's going on here?"

"Daddy!" Cassie was clearly excited to see him. "Grace let me have a tea party with my dolls. We shared a muffin and it's 'nanimous we won't spoil our appetites."

"Those muffins are pretty good." There was male appreciation in his eyes, the kind that was reserved for food.

The way to a man's heart is through his stomach.

Grace wished that saying hadn't popped into her head because it made her face flush. "I'm glad you liked them."

"It wasn't necessary for you to make them last night," he said.

She shrugged. "You had all the ingredients and I like to bake."

"I like to eat," Cassie chimed in.

Logan laughed. "It is kind of important."

"Daddy, you should have tea with us. It's only pretend, but Abigail and Hattie are too full to eat so they'll share with you." Her little face took on an earnest, pleading expression.

"Oh, honey, it looks like fun but—" He sighed "—I came up here because I have to eat lunch and then get back to work."

"But it's too early," she said.

"Not for me. I've been working since before the sun came up."

"While I was still sleepin'?"

He knelt on one knee beside her. "That's right."

"You must be tired. And really hungry," she said thoughtfully. "I have an idea."

"Oh?"

The tone was cautious, uneasy, and the look on his face said he'd rather walk barefoot on boulders than hear what his daughter was going to suggest.

"You should bring your lunch outside and we'll keep you company. Me and Abigail and Hattie and Grace."

Grace watched his reaction closely and couldn't quite put it in the fear category, but there was a definite dash of discomfort there.

"I sure wish I could, honey. But I have a busy afternoon and I need to eat quick."

"But, Daddy, it won't take that long."

"Maybe next time."

"Ookay." There was disappointment in her voice along with a measure of acceptance, as if the suggestion had been a long shot in the first place. Clearly she'd been turned down before.

"I'm really sorry." He held out his arms and without hesitation the little girl stood and moved into them, sliding her arms around his neck.

When his hold slackened, Cassie stepped away and looked at him a little sadly. "When I hug you, you always let go first."

"Do I?"

Grace didn't believe Cassie intended to hurt his feelings, but the words had sliced into him and hit their mark. It was clear by the tortured look in his eyes.

She really felt his pain and wanted so badly to say that five or ten minutes wouldn't make a difference to the horses and cows but could mean everything to his child. She opened her mouth, and he happened to be looking right at her.

A muscle jerked in his jaw. "Something on your mind?"

Just in time, she closed off the words and shook her head.

"Okay, then." He smiled at Cassie. "I'll see you tonight."

"Okay." She watched wistfully as he disappeared inside. "Mommy says the very best hugs are the 'never let go' kind."

"I know what she means, sweetie." And that's all she could say really.

Because it wasn't in her job description to comment on the father/daughter relationship, no matter how much she was tempted.

* * *

Logan was pretty sure Grace thought he was the lowest life-form on the planet for not joining the tea party yesterday. She'd almost said something but then checked the words, and he was glad she'd kept them to herself. Except he hadn't been able to get her disapproving look out of his mind. She wasn't very good at hiding her feelings, but he had his reasons—and they were good ones.

He'd been a kid living in a car with his younger siblings when he figured out that behind his mother's optimistic mask was fear. And that was his father's fault. No, he knew Grace's opinion of him ranged somewhere between snake and slimy single-cell organism. He'd had a dream last night and no expert was needed to analyze it. She'd pointed an accusing finger at him and before she could tell him he was a terrible father, he kissed her. That woke him up, and from then on it wasn't a restful sleep, which made a man crabby, short-tempered and careless.

He was in the barn repairing tack when he heard the sound of female voices just outside. One was Cassie's. The other was sexy and sweet, and he knew it belonged to Grace. Then his stomach clenched. Something was wrong or they wouldn't be here.

He left the little room where tack was stored and hurried to meet them in the hay-scattered main aisle that separated the rows of horse stalls. "What's going on?"

Grace frowned at his tone, but Cassie seemed unfazed. She ran up to him, her eyes bright with excitement.

"Hi, Daddy!" She was dressed in denim shorts and a pink T-shirt. Her hair was in some complicated weave. "Grace French-braided my hair. Isn't it pretty?"

"Beautiful." He looked at the woman standing beside the little girl and could have said the same thing. Her hair was pulled up in a sassy ponytail that brushed the shoulder of her skinny-strap shirt. Her shorts were black and revealed smooth, tanned skin that made his stomach clench again, for a very different reason. Beautiful.

"I was tellin' Grace about the cats and goats, so we came to see 'em." She ran past him and peeked into each of the empty stalls.

"Be careful," he said.

"I will."

He followed her and watched as she inspected every corner of the barn without success.

"Snowflake must be outside. I'm gonna go look," she said, then raced toward the wide opening and disappeared.

"Cassie—" Either she didn't hear or chose to ignore him. "I'm going after her."

"I'll go, but could you tag along? I'd like to speak with you about something."

"Okay." They walked to the open barn door and he saw his daughter looking around a bale of hay.

"She's just exploring. This won't take long, Logan. Promise."

"She needs eyes on her." The knot in his stomach tightened.

"Agreed. But this is a ranch, not a razor blade factory." Grace's mouth pulled tight for a moment and there was stubbornness in her expression, a clue that she wasn't going to back off on this. "Please, talk to me. I have some questions and need clarification."

He met her gaze and mentally braced himself. "Okay."

"Good." Her smile was polite, but something simmered beneath it. She looked at his daughter as she said, "For starters, I need to know what is and isn't okay to do with Cassie."

"That's your job. To know how to take care of her. It's why I hired you. For your judgment."

"That's what I thought, too." Flecks of gold were scattered in her hazel eyes and started to glow, the only hint they might shoot fire any second.

"Good, then we're finished here."

"Not quite. The thing is, I used my good judgment this morning. Cassie wanted to show me the baby goats and see if the cat had her babies. My judgment told me that would be fun for her, but I'm sensing that you don't agree, because you're acting as if we cut the stirrups off your favorite saddle."

Very perceptive. "She's five and has a lot of toys. Isn't that fun?"

"As you said—she's five, and that means she has a short attention span. This is a ranch. They're harmless animals." Her gaze slid from his to where Cassie was crouched down looking at a rock and poking it with a stick she'd picked up. So much for all the toys.

Why did she have to be so damn logical? And so sexy while she was doing it? "Cats scratch. Goats get frisky."

"Very true. And that's why I'm here to watch." Her gaze narrowed on his before looking at Cassie again. "But I'm sensing you disapprove of my decision. So I have to ask—what are approved activities?"

"Ones where she can't fall off a fence or wander too close to a horse and get kicked and hurt."

"So, indoor play only?"

"Exactly." Good. That was actually easier than he'd expected. Then he saw the defiant look in her eyes and he figured the laser beams were charging. "What?"

"I'm curious."

Curiosity killed the cat. If he didn't miss his guess, this was a trap set for him to step in and snap the jaws shut. "About?"

"Cassie visits with you here on the ranch almost every

weekend. So, how do you fill the time? What do you do for fun?"

He thought for a moment and saw no downside to telling her. "I take her to movies. Into Blackwater Lake for ice cream. There's a mall about forty-five minutes to an hour away and she likes to shop."

"So, all of the things you do together are indoors?"

"Not all." But he was starting to sweat. "We sit outside and eat the ice cream when the weather is nice."

Grace folded her arms over her chest. "How do you get any work done if you can't let her out of your sight?"

"When she's here I arrange my work schedule so that I'm free to be with her."

Her eyes widened. "I'm going to take a wild guess and say that this is the longest stretch of time you've had your daughter living with you."

Logan had helped her lay out all the dots, so it shouldn't come as a shock that a smart woman like her would connect them. "It works."

Grace blew out a long breath. "Why don't you just roll her up in Bubble Wrap or put her in biocontainment?"

"You're saying I'm overprotective." It wasn't a question. Cassie's mom told him that on a regular basis.

"I'd call it cautious. But why to this extent? Even the way your visits are structured, she's spent a lot of time here. She's old enough to know the rules, where to play and what's off-limits."

"Kids don't always follow directions and stay where they're supposed to."

"Can't argue with that. So, she's never out of your sight?"

"Never. And now you're here to do that when I can't."

He dragged his fingers through his hair. "Look, when she's with me it's my responsibility to make sure that no harm comes to her. The only thing that matters is Cassie.

Her happiness and well-being. I want her safe and will do whatever is necessary to see that she is. Isn't that what a father does?"

Logan really wanted to know because his own father didn't think about anyone but himself. It didn't take an advanced degree in early childhood education to know that wasn't right.

"Of course a father is supposed to do that." Grace's expression softened. It was as if she sensed he was no good at this and felt sorry for his daughter. Or worse, she pitied *him*. "And a mother, too. But—"

He held up a hand to stop her. "There's a word that strikes fear into a person's heart."

"It's just a three-letter word." Her mouth twitched as if she wanted to laugh.

"Uh-huh." Let her make fun. It was better than feeling sorry for him. "That word is a signal. It means you're not going to like the rest of what's coming."

"This is worth what you paid for it." She did smile then and moved farther away from the barn entrance to see the little girl who'd wandered out of view as she explored. "Come to think of it, you are paying me. But Cassie is your child and I will care for her however you want, to the very best of my ability. This is just food for thought. You obviously love her very much. Just keep in mind that rigidly controlling her environment will keep her physically safe but could squeeze the joy out of her soul."

Just then the little girl in question came running around the corner of the barn straight toward them. "Grace!"

She crouched down as the child stopped in front of her, breathing hard from the exertion. She studied the eager expression. "What, sweetie?"

"I found Snowflake. She made a home in some hay and has babies. Come and see!"

"Okay." Grace grinned and Cassie grabbed the hand she held out.

"Bye, Daddy!"

"Be careful. See you later, baby girl."

There was no push back on the endearment because his daughter was mission driven as she dragged Grace away.

Logan should have breathed a sigh of relief that the pretty lady was gone. Instead he felt uneasy. Maybe with a touch of disappointment mixed in. Cassie hadn't insisted on showing him the kittens and he felt a little left out. It made him wonder just whose soul was in jeopardy.

Damn it.

His life had been working just fine until Grace Flynn walked into it. End of summer was a long way off and couldn't come too soon as far as he was concerned. And not just because Cassie would be safely back with her mother again.

It meant Mary Poppins would be gone and his world would go back to normal. She'd been here only a couple days, but she had a way about her, one that messed with his head. Women had told him off before, but not one of them was as hot and sexy as Grace when she did it.

That was new, and no one liked change. Especially him.

Chapter Three

"Grace has to come with us to Fourth of July, Daddy." Cassie Hunt stood in the kitchen and looked up at her father with hope and determination on her cute-as-a-button face.

Grace was watching Logan's reaction, and it was awfully hard to keep from laughing. He didn't know how to respond. This was a holiday, and even a hardworking rancher like him was taking some time off. It was late afternoon, and Cassie had told her they were going into Blackwater Lake for the celebration. Grace had said she hoped they had a good time, and the little girl insisted she had to come along, then confronted her father.

"The truth is, Cassie, I've been so busy I forgot to ask Grace about it," he said honestly. "I will fix that right now. Grace, would you like to go with us for the Fourth of July celebration?"

"Thanks for asking, but it's all right." Being included felt like crossing a line from professional to personal. And from what he'd said about being only a weekend dad, this was a good chance for the two of them to hang out by themselves. "I don't want to intrude on your time together."

"But you hafta come," Cassie pleaded. "It's fun. And there's a parade."

"What else is going on?" she asked.

"Hot dogs. Pizza. And cotton candy." The little girl thought for a moment. "There's rides and fireworks. I don't like the real loud ones, though."

"All of that sounds good except the cotton candy. If that's a deal breaker…"

"You don't have to eat it," Logan said. "You should come with us. We're celebrating America's independence, and it's downright un-American to sit here by yourself." He settled his hands on lean hips. "If you were in Buckskin Pass what would you be doing?"

There she would go to the annual town celebration and try not to smack Lance the Loser, who had broken her heart and her bank account. In her current situation, being by herself meant not having to pretend she wasn't infatuated with this cowboy. When she was around him, the attraction meter never failed to click into the danger zone.

"I would take part in the Buckskin Pass festivities," she finally admitted, leaving out the part about Lance the Loser.

"Then you should come with us." Was that guilt, reluctance or obligation in his tone?

"Daddy's right."

"Wow." He looked at his daughter as if she was an alien being from another planet. "That hardly ever happens. Me? Correct about something? That parade today just might be in my honor."

"You have to, Grace. I'll be sad if you don't." Cassie thrust out her bottom lip in an unmistakable pout.

Grace sighed. "Who can resist that face? Not me, that's for sure."

"Yay!"

At least one out of three was pleased. Grace thought Logan looked as if his horses had just gone on strike. In spite of his inviting her along, his body language said he didn't want to be around her any more than necessary.

Actually, she couldn't blame him. It's what she deserved after offering unsolicited parenting advice in her first couple of days on the job. Now she was barely into week number two. She'd made a personal vow not to offer an opinion unless he asked for it.

"How does my hair look, Daddy?"

"I like the ribbons. Red, white and blue. Very patriotic."

"Grace did it." She turned her head from side to side, showing off the ponytail and the long strands of ribbon decorating it. "I'm never getting my hair cut."

"That's a topic best discussed with your mom." He looked at Grace. "You ready to go?"

She glanced at her denim capri pants and red T-shirt with stars and stripes. If only there was an anti-Logan spray like the one you could buy to repel mosquitoes. Not to say he was a pest, but it would come in handy. Alas, no such product existed. "I'll just get my purse and light jackets for Cassie and me."

A little while later Logan drove into a lot designated for holiday parking because Main Street Blackwater Lake was closed off to through traffic. The carnival rides were operating in the same open area, and Cassie's eyes grew wider as she pointed out the ones she wanted to go on.

Logan made no comment but kept on walking. It was a short distance to the parade area, and they looked around to find the best viewing spot in the crowd gathered up and down the street. As it turned out, all the front-row spaces were taken and the audience was several people deep. Before they could decide where to go, she heard someone call out Logan's name.

"Look!" Cassie pointed at the Grizzly Bear Diner. "There's Uncle Tucker and Uncle Max and Aunt Jamie."

"My siblings," Logan explained.

"A big family." Grace envied him. She had no one, except the friends she'd made in Buckskin Pass. Although she'd made the comment that it must have been fun growing up with them, his response had been "not really." Why did she get the feeling that circumstances and not his brothers and sister had colored his view? "They look nice."

"You might change your mind about that after you meet them. There's no getting out of this now that we've been spotted." His voice was teasing. In spite of the words, he looked pleased to see them. "Brace for impact."

Cassie took both of their hands and tugged them through the crowd to where the three siblings stood together. "Hi!"

"Hello, peanut." The pretty twentysomething woman bent to hug her niece. "Love your holiday hair."

"I know. I love it, too. Grace did it."

Questioning blue eyes, a lot like Logan's, regarded her. "And you must be Grace, the hair goddess."

"Be nice, Jamie. Don't scare her off." Logan put his hand at the small of her back. "This is Grace Flynn. She's taking care of Cassie for the summer."

"Tracy mentioned she was hiring someone to help while she plans for the wedding then goes on her honeymoon." The woman's look was friendly and welcoming.

"Grace," Logan continued, "this is my sister, Jamie Hart, and my brothers, Tucker and Max Hart."

All of them Harts? But Logan's last name was Hunt. Maybe they were half siblings, she thought, although some instinct told her that wasn't the case. The family resemblance, especially among the men, was pretty strong. All three were better-than-average-looking and would have women sacrificing to the matchmaking gods.

"It's nice to meet you all." She shook hands with each of them. His brother Max was tall and broad, like a walking mountain, and his big hand swallowed hers. "You look familiar," she said.

"If you recognize him it's probably from tabloid stories linking him to all his groupies. He played in the National Hockey League," Logan explained.

Grace decided to ignore the not very veiled reference to women. "Played? Past tense?"

"Ankle injury. It affected my skating skills." Max shrugged, and his dark blue eyes didn't reveal how he felt about a career-ending injury.

"Now he has too much time on his hands and uses it to harass me." Tucker was tall, muscular and somewhere in his thirties. He was pretty cute, too. "I have better things to do than prop up his ego."

"Building houseboats is no big deal," Max shot back.

"What are you guys? Five? Our niece is more mature than you," their sister teased.

Grace had always wished for a big brother, and this woman had three to protect her. She envied that. "What do you do, Jamie?"

"She's a nurse practitioner and works at Mercy Medical Clinic here in town." Logan's voice and expression were full of pride and affection. "Our little sister saves lives."

"She gives shots." Cassie wrinkled her freckled nose.

"I've never given one to you," her aunt said. "And if I did, it would be because an injection was medically necessary."

"Does that mean only if I really and truly needed it?"

"Yes." Jamie hugged her tight. "You're so smart, my pretty little peanut."

"Breaking news. The parade is starting." Because he was the tallest, Max could see over the heads of all the people in front of them.

"I can't see anything," Cassie complained.

"That can be fixed." Her very big uncle scooped her up and settled her on his wide shoulders. "How's that?"

"I can see better than anyone!" The little girl squealed with delight.

Grace was shifting to get a better view of the street,

and her arm brushed Logan's. The tingles commenced as if the starting buzzer had just sounded at a track meet. Just when she managed to get a handle on the feeling, he put his hands on her arms and urged her to stand in front of him.

"You can see better here," he said.

His touch was gentle, but his fingers on her bare skin felt hot enough to leave a mark. It was only the space of a heartbeat before he dropped his hands, but she missed the contact. That was weird, along with the fact that his brothers were extraordinarily good-looking men, but neither of them made her toes curl like Logan did.

Then the Blackwater Lake High School band marched by playing "America the Beautiful," distracting her from the unsettling reaction. For about fifteen minutes she watched horses, antique cars and even a covered wagon go by. At the end of the line was the town fire department's big red hook and ladder. A very handsome, dark-haired firefighter stood on the running board, waving an American flag.

"He's cute," Grace commented.

"Never judge a book by its cover," Jamie muttered.

The tone and words convinced Grace that Logan's sister had a Lance the Loser story, too.

"You should give him a break, Jamie. Des Parker isn't a bad guy." Tucker gently nudged his sister's shoulder.

She gave him a look that would melt steel. "Do you really want to give me advice on the opposite sex, Tucker? You spent years living with a woman and couldn't cross the finish line." Jamie leaned toward Grace and whispered loud enough to be heard in the next county, "No one knows why that long-term relationship ended, but it makes his qualifications for offering romantic advice questionable."

Logan gave his brother a sympathetic look. "I hate to say it, Tuck, but she's got a point."

"Really?" The brother in question shook his head. "You're taking her side?"

"Look at it this way," the cowboy said. "I will never need a houseboat, what with living on the ranch and all. But at some point, medical care is a real possibility. This is a strategic decision about which one of you I can least afford to tick off."

Grace cracked up. "You guys are too funny."

"Logan," his sister told him, "I always knew you were wise beyond your years, and you get points for that. But the truth is that men are pigs. Am I right, Grace?"

Now she was on the spot. It was three against three if you counted Cassie, but she was too young to know anything about being hurt by a man. "I'm not comfortable labeling all of them that way. Especially when three of them are standing right here and one is my boss. But—" she glanced at Logan, remembering how he felt about that particular word "—I'm pretty sure a majority of women have a pig in their past."

Jamie nodded knowingly. "You and I need to talk sometime."

"About what?" Cassie demanded.

"Grown-up stuff." Grace felt guilty that her comment had slipped out and wished she could rewind and delete. She glanced at Logan, his brown Stetson shading his eyes, and caught something dark and intense in his expression. At least she thought so. It disappeared as soon as their gazes touched.

"Not to change this fascinating subject," Max interjected, "but Bar None has a beer booth set up across the street. I think we should go get one."

"I don't like beer," Cassie said.

"Do I want to know how and why you know that?" Tucker asked his niece.

"I just know," his niece declared. "Because I want to go and play the beanbag game."

Grace could tell Logan was conflicted about what to do and figured she could help him out. "You go with your family. I'll take Cassie to see the games."

"You're not on duty. It's a holiday," he protested.

"I like hanging out with her. It's not work." She saw his hesitation and said, "Look, we can debate the issue and waste time until everyone is bored to tears—"

"I'm already bored," Cassie chimed in. She pointed at someone nearby. "There's my friend Lindsay. I wanna go play."

"I rest my case. So you can give in—dare I say it— gracefully and everyone gets what they want," she said.

"Not only is Grace pretty," Max said, "she's right. It would be best to go with her on this, big brother."

Logan glared at everyone in general, but before he could respond, Cassie piped up.

"Daddy, *please* can I go with Grace?"

He thought for a moment, then finally nodded. "Okay, kiddo. But you stay with her."

As if the little girl weighed nothing, Max lifted her from his shoulders and set her on her feet. "There you go, munchkin."

"Thanks, Uncle Max. I'm goin' over there to see my friend Lindsay." She ran over and the two girls hugged.

"I guess that's settled." Logan slid his fingers into his jeans pockets.

"It was nice to meet you all," Grace said.

"Likewise." Max gave her a charming grin. "My brother doesn't deserve you. But it's good to know my niece is in expert hands."

"One beer," Logan told her. "I'll call your cell to see where the two of you are when I'm finished."

"Okay."

She watched the four of them start across the street, then turned away when there was a tug on her hand. "What is it?"

"Grace, can I go on the roller coaster with Lindsay? Her mom and dad are comin' with us. Please?"

"Okay, I'll just tag along—"

"Hold on." Logan came up behind her. "I thought you were taking her to play the games."

Grace's eyes were on Cassie, who drifted back to her friend's family, out of hearing distance. Then she glanced up at her tense and decidedly displeased employer. "She changed her mind. It happens when you're a five-year-old girl. She wants to go on a ride with her friend and parents."

"We didn't talk about this," he said.

"You hired me to use my own judgment," she reminded him. "But if you don't trust me—"

"It's not that." He rubbed a hand across the back of his neck. "I just feel as if I should be there."

Be there? Really? She'd vowed not to offer advice, but technically she wasn't. "If being there is so important, why didn't you take ten minutes to sit and have a pretend tea party with her?"

"I'm not good at that." Uncertainty mixed with the tension on his face. "And don't ask me to explain how or why, but this is different."

Grace searched his gaze for several moments, not exactly sure what she was looking for but convinced she wasn't finding any answers there. "Do you want me to tell her she can't go on the ride?"

He shook his head. "I'll take her."

"But your family is waiting for you," she protested.

"They'll live." He looked down for a moment, then back

at her. "And so we're clear, I do trust you. This is on me, not you."

Without another word, Logan walked over to where Cassie was with her friend's family. He shook hands and smiled at Lindsay's parents in a casual, friendly way before the group threaded through the crowd in the direction of the open area where the carnival rides were set up.

Grace saw the protective hand he put on his daughter's small shoulder, and the sight tugged at her heart. He was the personification of the strong, silent, solid cowboy—polite and protective. She believed him when he said he trusted her but would bet almost anything that he didn't trust himself.

Why was that?

Unlike his daughter, who'd conked out in the truck on the way home after fireworks, Logan couldn't sleep when they got back to the ranch. He was tossing and turning in bed and couldn't get Grace off his mind. For a lot of reasons, not the least of which was the feel of her bare skin beneath his hands. But mostly it was how she'd looked at him when he got squirrelly about Cassie going on a carnival ride without him there to watch her. You'd think he set Grace's hot-pink panties on fire.

Well, maybe that wasn't the best way to think of it since he was the one with hot pants and doing his damnedest not to let on. No, that look of hers was about judging him, and in the fatherhood department, he came up short. Trying to hide the fact that he had no idea what he was doing wasn't working. She was too good with kids not to see the truth. Before she came here, things with him and Cassie were fine. Weekends were sacred, and the hired help took over. He hung out with his daughter, and when she was with him, he knew she was safe. He didn't have to delegate that responsibility.

Now he had to trust Grace with what was most precious to him in this world. But trust didn't come easy. The fact was, he'd never hated Foster Hart more than he did at this moment. Thanks to that bastard, he had no blueprint of what a good father looked like.

Logan heard something, and his eyes popped open, adrenaline pumping. The sound came again, and he realized it was Cassie crying out. He threw off the covers and jumped out of bed, his only thought to get to her.

He ran down the hall and saw that her bedroom door was open, and faint light from her lamp spilled out. Inside, Grace sat on the bed cradling the little girl in her arms. Since her room was next to Cassie's, she got there first and was crooning comforting words.

"It was a bad dream, honey. You're fine. I'm here. There's nothing to be afraid of, I promise." She met his gaze, and there was a question in her eyes.

Logan knew she was wondering if he wanted to take over, and he shook his head. Cassie was clinging to Grace, and he figured she was probably better off right where she was.

"It's okay, sweetheart." The sobs were tapering off as Grace rocked her and rubbed her back. "Do you want to talk about it?"

"I'll be scared." Cassie clutched even tighter.

"Sometimes if we share something that scares us it loses the power to be frightening."

"Somethin' was after me." Cassie sniffled. "I ran and ran as fast as I could, but it grabbed my shirt and I couldn't get away. I kept saying, 'Help,' but nobody came."

"Oh, honey." Grace brushed a hand over Cassie's hair.

"I'm so sorry you were scared. It was just a dream, though, and can't hurt you. I'm here. Your dad is here."

Cassie lifted her head and looked at him. "I didn't see you, Daddy. Sorry I waked you up."

"It's okay, baby girl. Are you okay?"

"Better now." She yawned. "Do I hafta go back to sleep? I don't want to."

"Not until you're ready," Grace assured her. "I'll be here with you, okay?"

"I know." The little girl nodded and relaxed against Grace again.

Logan had heard that kids had an instinct about people and didn't suffer fools. If that was true, Cassie completely trusted this woman, and he was relieved about that. In a perfect world, no one would ever let this little girl down. The irony was that a kid's father should be the first line of defense, but Logan worried that he was the one most likely to disappoint her.

When Cassie yawned again, Grace asked, "Do you want to go back to bed?"

Cassie nodded and crawled out of her lap beneath the covers, then grabbed the stuffed bear Logan had bought her on one of their mall trips. Grace reached over and turned out the light but not before he caught a glimpse of her in the flimsy flowered pajamas she wore to bed. His body went tight and hard, proving how much he wanted her. If he needed any, it was more proof of how much he was like his father. He was lusting after the childcare professional while his little girl was in the middle of a meltdown.

Cassie whimpered. "I'm scared."

"I'm here." Grace stretched out on the bed and pulled the child against her. "Tell me what you're afraid of."

"There's a monster on my ceiling."

Grace looked up. "The shadows?"

"Uh-huh."

Between the moon's rays streaming through the princess curtains and the night-light plugged into an outlet, a whole bunch of shadows were hovering above the bed. The only way to make them disappear was to leave the light on, and Logan was just about to suggest that. Then Grace started talking in her soft, sweet, soothing tone. He wished he could see her because when she used this voice there was always something innocent in her eyes that he liked.

"I don't see a monster on the ceiling. It looks like an elephant to me, a cute and cuddly one." She pointed. "There's his trunk and big, floppy ears. Can you make it out?"

"Yes," Cassie said.

"Or maybe a fairy—like Tinker Bell. There are the little wings and her arms stretched out for flying."

"I can see her."

Grace pointed again. "I think that could be an ice-cream cone. See the pointy part and the mound on top?"

"Uh-huh." Cassie's yawn was long, and her mouth stretched wide open. "In the corner I see a ladybug. There's the round body and tiny wings when she flies away."

"Good one."

Between his daughter's yawn and her getting involved in finding friendly shapes in the ceiling shadows, Logan knew the crisis was winding down. Grace had managed the situation without resorting to keeping the light on. He backed out of the doorway but stayed in the hall, listening to the low voices that soon became just one—Grace's.

Eventually she tiptoed out and looked startled when she saw him, the same expression she'd worn when he scared her into dropping her panties while unpacking.

"I thought you went back to bed," she whispered.

"No."

"You could have." Based on the hushed voice, it was hard to tell whether or not her tone was defensive.

"I stayed—just in case."

"Everything is under control. And I assume you have to get up before God to work in the morning."

"Yeah."

"Then I have to conclude that you don't trust me."

"Not you, Grace. It's me I don't trust."

"I kind of figured that. In town. Cassie and the carnival ride clued me in."

"Yeah."

"You act like a bodyguard, and I mean that literally. In order to be sure she's physically all right, you can't let her out of your sight. But you don't want to get down and play with her. Why are you putting that distance between you? Do you want to talk about it?"

Just minutes ago she'd told Cassie that sharing something you're scared of can make it lose the power to be frightening. Maybe she was right. For reasons he didn't understand, Logan was going to tell her.

"Yeah," he said. "I do want to talk about it."

Chapter Four

Logan wanted to talk about this so Grace would stop looking at him as if he was winning the Worst Dad of the Century award in a landslide. If she understood how screwed up his childhood had been, she would get that he was doing this for Cassie.

"Grace, I—"

She put a finger to her lips to stop him and angled her head toward the open door to his daughter's room. In a whisper she said, "Let's go downstairs. I'm going to grab a robe."

He felt a stab of disappointment at the prospect of her doing anything to cover up that sweet shape. Yet another shred of proof about his being messed up in general and not just his dad skills.

Then her gaze dropped to his bare chest for a moment and something flashed in her eyes. He might not know how to be a dad, but he knew female appreciation when he saw it. Too bad that made his ego feel better because other parts of him felt pretty damn lousy.

"I'll put on a shirt," he said.

Logan did that, then went downstairs. He'd barely flipped on the lights when he felt Grace behind him. She was tying the belt of her short satiny robe, and darned if that wasn't sexy as hell.

"Do you want a drink?" he asked.

"Water."

"I was thinking something stronger." Even though he knew there wasn't enough Scotch in the world to take the edge off the crap of how his childhood played out.

"You go ahead," she said.

He shook his head. "Water it is."

After getting two glasses and filling them with filtered water from the fridge, they sat down at the kitchen table facing each other.

Grace took a sip, then wrapped her hands around the glass. "So, talk. I'm listening."

No point in sugarcoating this. "My father is a bastard."

She blinked, but otherwise her expression didn't change. "I'm going to take a wild guess. You mean that as an indictment of his character and not about his being born out of wedlock."

"You would be correct. My paternal grandparents are good people. Salt of the earth. Their other son, Hastings—"

"Your uncle."

"Yes." He had cousins, too, here in Blackwater Lake. They'd reached out, but Logan wasn't wired to jump in with both feet, *because* they were family. "Anyway, Hastings is the kind of son every parent would be proud of. A loving husband and father. Never gave his folks a bit of trouble. And then there was Foster."

"Your dad."

Dad? Logan never thought of him that way. The term was intimate and implied a level of commitment and caring to earn the name.

"My father is the complete opposite of his brother. Uninvolved with his family and unfaithful to his wife. Beats me why he proposed to my mother at all since he didn't stop seeing other women even after they were engaged."

"Well, that really stinks."

The anger on her face was better than pity. "He had affairs and mistresses and kids with more than one of them."

"You have half siblings?"

"They're around."

"That boggles the mind. I don't understand—"

"Join the club."

"No," she said. "I meant why didn't your parents just get a divorce?"

"The better question is why he ever got married in the first place." He thought for a moment. "I don't have confirmation, but I have a guess about that."

"Shoot."

"He was looking for the same kind of approval from his parents that Hastings already had. Foster got tired of hearing about his older brother's beautiful wife and family and wanted his share of the parental approval pie."

"So he proposed to your mom. I guess she had no idea he was a cheater."

"Not then. And she got pregnant with me right away. When she found out he was sleeping around, it was a lot harder to walk away with a baby. And he didn't want the sordid truth to trash his new image with the folks." The disgust that tightened inside him was like an old friend. "To keep her from leaving he pulled out every cliché. No points for originality. He told her he loved her and was sorry. It would never happen again. So she stayed, and there was no need for anyone else to know."

"Your mother believed him." It wasn't a question, and the hostile expression in her eyes was a clue that she'd had her own experience with a rat-bastard liar. "Your dad must be a smooth talker."

"Yes. And the truth is that she didn't want to leave. Not really. She actually loved him."

"Hard to believe." Grace's lips pressed together.

"Yeah. But that wasn't enough for him. The cheating didn't stop. Neither did the clichés. His smooth talking worked after Tucker, Max and Jamie."

"But she finally did leave. What made her pull the trigger on that?"

"He got one of his mistresses pregnant. Probably more, but this woman called my mother and told her to let him go. He didn't love her and she should set him free so he could be happy with her and their baby."

"Oh, my God. What nerve. Your mother must have been enraged."

Logan remembered how his mom looked after that phone conversation. All the color had drained from her face, and she was completely shocked. There was fear and hurt in her eyes but no fury.

He shook his head. "No anger. She loved him until the day she died."

"Logan—" She gripped her water glass tighter. "I don't know what to say."

"It gets worse." He met her gaze but still saw no evidence that she was feeling sorry for him. "She was too humiliated to stay but didn't have anywhere to go. And she wouldn't ask the Harts for help."

"But this ranch—"

"It belonged to her father, and he had disowned her for marrying Foster. Granddad pegged him for a loser, but she refused to listen. When she had to leave, she wouldn't swallow her pride and go to her father."

"What happened? Where did you go?"

"We lived in the car."

"Four of you kids and your mother?"

He nodded. "She waited tables and cleaned houses but couldn't make enough to put a permanent roof over our heads. Sometimes we went to a homeless shelter. There was an occasional cheap motel room if tips were good."

"What about you kids?"

He knew what she was asking. "I took care of them."

Her eyes widened. "How old were you?"

"Twelve."

"Just a kid yourself," she said.

"Yeah." As much as he wanted to, there was no forgetting the humiliation and fear. He'd done his best to be the man of the family.

"Obviously your mom eventually contacted her father."

He nodded. "Jamie got really sick, and there was no choice. Granddad was really glad to hear from her. He'd missed her and had no idea we were living in a car. He took us in, and we stayed here on the ranch."

"It's a great place to grow up." She was studying him. "But an experience like that leaves a mark."

"Look, I didn't tell you all that to get the sympathy vote."

"I never thought you did. And I don't pity you."

He looked but didn't see any in her eyes, which was a relief. But he saw a lot of questions. "What?"

"You had a reason for talking about this to me, Logan."

"I want you to understand. I'm in over my head with Cassie. Being a father scared the hell out of me from the moment Tracy told me she was pregnant. I love my daughter more than anything, and I'm afraid of screwing her up somehow because I have no clue what a good father looks like."

"And yet you became the man of the family for your brothers and sister," she pointed out.

"Not the same thing. Her mom calls the shots and I see her on weekends. It's worked just fine." He blew out a breath. "Until now."

"Because you have her for more than two days."

"Yeah. And you think I'm holding on too tight. But the thing is, I know if I don't take my eyes off her she'll be physically safe. I can control that. The rest of it?" He shrugged. "One wrong move. One thoughtless word, and she could be as messed up as me."

"I think it would take more than that," she said wryly. "Have you considered therapy?"

"What?"

She looked dead serious for a moment, then the corners of her mouth curved up. "Logan, you just described every parent's worst fear. Imperfect people raise imperfect people. They just do the best they can, and it's enough. You are not unique. You are not predisposed to ruin your daughter's life."

"No?" Her lack of judgment lifted a weight from his shoulders. "And I thought I was special."

"Oh, please. Did you ever consider the fact that your grandfather was a role model? It wasn't a traditional family, of course, but he was there."

"I spent a lot of time with him learning about working the ranch."

"Something tells me you learned more than that. Maybe about being a good person?"

"I wouldn't count on that. My formative years were spent with Foster Hart."

"But the years you grew into a man happened here. Don't sell yourself short."

In for a penny, in for a pound, he thought. "Did I mention that my father frequently hit on the household staff?" He watched her face as that information sank in. "I caught him with one of the maids."

"Wow, he really is a piece of work. Never met a cliché he didn't embrace."

"You got it."

"I'm going to take another wild guess here." She tapped her lip. "You want to show the world that you're nothing like him and will not be hitting on an employee living under your roof."

He saw no reason not to confirm her theory. "You're right about that. No way you have anything to worry about from me."

"Well, you have no idea what a relief that is. Because every woman is dying to know that a handsome cowboy can resist her with no effort at all."

"I— Well—" He ran his fingers through his hair. Clearly being a father wasn't the only thing he was bad at. The twists and turns of a woman's mind were beyond him, too. "I didn't mean to offend you."

"I'm teasing." She smiled. "This was a good talk, and I'm not even going to charge you the going rate for therapy. And don't worry. Cassie is resilient. She can survive you. And I'm here to help navigate the waters."

"Okay. Good."

"It's late and you have to get up soon. Good night, Logan."

"Night."

When she was gone, he blew out a long breath. Obviously she didn't notice that resisting her was the hardest thing he'd ever done. With luck he could keep it that way.

Grace held Cassie's hand as they walked from the parking lot behind the Harvest Café to the back door of the restaurant where they were meeting her mother for lunch. The two were going to do wedding errands for the quickly approaching event.

Tracy was already seated at a table in the corner but stood and waved when she saw them come in. She hugged her daughter when the child ran into her arms.

"Hi, Mommy!"

"I've missed you, sweetie." Tracy Medeiros was a dark-haired beauty, and it was obvious why she'd caught Logan's eye once upon a time. Now this woman was the mother of his child and they were the gold standard for parenting without being partners. "Hi, Grace."

"How are you, Tracy?"

"Getting nervous about the wedding," she said as they all sat down at the table.

The café was done in fall colors of green, rust and gold. Country-themed pictures were on the walls, and a shelf near the ceiling held a metal pitcher, an old washboard and a milk can along with other similar decorations.

Grace put her cloth napkin in her lap. "Just so you know, there are bridezilla rumors."

"And I've been trying so hard to shut them down." The other woman laughed. "With Cassie's help today I'm hoping to put a big dent in my to-do list. Most of it is final approval on big stuff. Dress fittings for us, guest book, champagne glasses for Denver and me."

"That's a lot, Mom." The little girl frowned at the daunting list.

"It is," her mother agreed. "But I think it will go fast. It better because you and I have an appointment at the beauty salon for a wedding hairdo trial run and mani/pedis."

"Oh, boy!" Cassie's eyes sparkled at the mention of girlie stuff.

The waitress came over, introduced herself and took their orders—chef salads for the two women and chicken tenders from the children's menu for Cassie.

As they waited for their food, Grace asked questions about how Tracy wanted her daughter's time structured. Their philosophy on letting her be a carefree child was the same. Kindergarten would be starting soon, so if there was a way to incorporate learning activities in a fun way she was on board with that.

"At least once or twice a week I try to schedule playdates with her friends," Tracy said.

"Paige and Emily," Cassie interjected. "They're my best friends."

"We switch off houses so it's only every third week that one mom is responsible for all three. I've tried to work out a playdate at one of the other girls' houses for your afternoon off."

Grace figured that was about not inconveniencing a working rancher. "I'm trying to picture Logan in charge of snacks and activities for three five-year-old girls."

"I know." The thought amused Tracy, too. "His skill set runs more toward riding, roping and herding cattle."

"I don't see him as the doll-playing, tea-partying type either." In fact, Grace had seen the evidence for herself that he wasn't.

While they chatted, the waitress brought their food and drinks, then quietly left them to eat.

"Some of that is my fault." Tracy took a bite of her salad, then chewed and swallowed as she glanced at her daughter. Cassie was more interested in the small coloring book and crayons the waitress had brought than her food. Her mother sighed. "My name is Tracy and I'm an enabler."

"Oh?"

"When she was born, he was so in love with her and so in over his head. I just didn't have the heart to throw him into the deep end of the pool with an infant—changing diapers, nighttime feedings. And I was breastfeeding. He visited her every day and I was glad he did. We're good friends." She sipped her iced tea. "When she was potty-trained and comfortable being away from me, we fell into the routine of her being at his house on weekends."

"He told me he's never been on his own with her this long before." Grace speared some turkey and lettuce with her fork and ate it.

"Whenever I brought up the idea of splitting time with her, he looked like I was a two-headed alien from the planet Mars. I couldn't do that to either of them. Although I wanted to keep our arrangement fair and give him as much time with her as he wanted. He's paying child support, and it's generous. He's such a good guy."

"A good guy? That sounds like something I want to know about." The pretty, blue-eyed blonde who stopped by their table was wearing a white chef's jacket. That was a big clue that she'd put together their food. "Who are we talking about, ladies?"

"Cassie's father," Tracy said. "This is the best salad, Lucy. And you know I'd rather have your gourmet burger, but I'm making sacrifices so I can fit into my wedding dress."

"Hmm. Maybe I'll call that salad 'the bridal gown greens.'" She looked at Grace. "I'm Lucy Bishop, by the way. Half owner of the Harvest Café."

"Grace Flynn," she said. "Nice to meet you. And this is a really good salad."

"Grace is here to take care of Cassie while I get ready for the wedding, then go on the honeymoon with my honey."

Lucy was looking at Grace, but in a conspiratorial whisper she said to Cassie, "Do we like her?"

"Yes. Grace makes blueberry muffins for my tea parties and we look at elephant shadows on the ceiling when I get scared at night."

At the woman's puzzled look, Grace added, "It makes perfect sense in context."

"I'll have to take your word for that," the chef said. "And speaking of good men... Have you met Tucker Hart?"

"Yes. The day before yesterday at the Fourth of July parade," Grace answered. "Max and Jamie were there, too."

"There's something in the Hart genes." The other woman sighed. "Those are some exceptionally nice-looking men."

"My daddy is handsome," Cassie said, catching the drift of the comments.

"Yes, he is, honey," Lucy agreed. "And your uncle Max is not hard on the eyes and like a big kid. And how lucky is he? Getting well paid to play a game. Uncle Tucker is awfully cute, too. And funny."

"Tucker came back to town recently," Tracy explained. "He builds houseboats and has traveled all over the country. Now he's here because his grandfather left him a good-sized parcel of waterfront property on Blackwater Lake and he finally has the time to come home and build a community there."

Grace envied the Harts. Yes, there'd been a rough patch when their mom split from their father but they landed with family who cared. They had roots and each other. A connection like that was something Grace had always wanted and would never have.

"That sounds like an exciting venture," she said.

"Tucker's pretty jazzed about it." Lucy appeared to be personally invested.

"Seems like you've gotten to know Tucker pretty well." Tracy had clearly noticed the more-than-friendly-interest tone, too.

"He's a bachelor who doesn't cook and comes in here to eat a lot." Lucy's exaggerated shrug seemed to be overdoing the indifference just a little. "We talk. He's friendly. I like him."

"Oh?" There was a tell-me-more twinkle in Tracy's dark eyes.

"It's not what you're thinking. And just because your

head is filled with glitter and sparkle and happily-ever-afters, that doesn't mean anyone else wants all that shiny stuff. Am I right, Grace?"

"I couldn't agree more." When the other woman held up a hand for a high five, Grace accommodated her.

"See?" Lucy looked satisfied. "Someone else knows that glitter just leaves a mess to clean up and you can never quite get rid of it."

"Have you ever heard that expression about protesting too much?" Tracy looked at both of them, then settled her gaze on Lucy. "I'm just saying that you show all the signs of having a soft spot for Tucker Hart."

"And all I'm saying is that he seems like a really good guy," Lucy protested. "Someone should marry him."

"Aha." Tracy's tone was full of gotcha.

"I didn't say anything about *me* marrying him. But Blackwater Lake is full of single women, and he could have his pick. A woman could do worse."

Grace figured that, just like herself, Lucy had her reasons for not wanting to get involved with a man. She planned to buy a house and put down roots in Buckskin Pass, and nothing was going to sidetrack her. Especially a man.

"It's getting hotter out here than my kitchen," Lucy said cheerfully. "I think I'll go back to it. Miss Cassie, would you care to come with me? I'm sure I can interest you in some dessert that just came out of the oven."

"Is it chocolate cake?" When the other woman smiled and nodded, Cassie turned pleading eyes on Tracy. "Can I, Mommy? Please."

"Of course."

The little girl slid off her chair and took the hand Lucy held out. Together they walked toward the kitchen.

Now that they were alone, Grace didn't have to choose

her words carefully. There were things she wanted to know, and now was a chance to find out.

"I'm assuming you know all about Logan's life before settling with his grandfather here in Blackwater Lake."

Tracy nodded. "I can't imagine living in a car with my child."

"He told me because I noticed that he carries the over-protective thing to a whole new level."

"I worry about that," the other woman admitted. "Cassie is only five and isn't pushing back on it yet. But she will. If he doesn't loosen up by the time she's a teenager, there's no telling how her rebellion will look or what kind of fall-out there will be."

"Have you met his father?"

"Yes." Tracy frowned. "Logan's cousin got married last summer, and Foster was there. Charming man. Hard to believe he was such a toad to his wife and kids. But people change."

"The way Logan looked when he talked about him…" Grace remembered the dark intensity in his eyes. The loathing that was palpable.

"Logan believes he could be like his father."

"And if he doesn't maintain rigid control over everything his inner toad will get loose," Grace guessed.

"That's what I think, too." Tracy sighed. "I just wish he could relax and enjoy his daughter. He's missing out on so much by holding himself back."

"Maybe there's some glitter here, besides your wedding, I mean. Because of the situation, he's spending eight weeks with Cassie. Putting in the time is really the only way he's going to feel more comfortable being a father."

"I hope you're right."

Grace had been curious about something else and just decided to come out and ask. Tracy seemed to be pretty forthcoming about their relationship. "I have a question, and feel free to tell me to mind my own business."

"Okay."

"You and Logan get along so great, I can't help wondering why you didn't get married."

Clearly not offended, Tracy smiled at the question. "When I got pregnant he proposed."

"Obviously you said no."

"Actually I laughed first."

"Ouch," Grace said.

"I wasn't making fun. He was very sweet and trying to do the right thing. Which is why it's so stupid that he's afraid of being like his father." Tracy's smile disappeared. "The truth is that we're better off as friends. He agreed— was actually relieved, I think. I want him in my life, as my friend and my daughter's father. But it would never have worked out if he was my husband."

"Why?"

"He'll never let himself fall in love, and I wasn't prepared to settle for less than that."

"I see."

Love ruined his mother's life, and he wasn't going to give it a chance to do the same to him. She knew the other woman didn't mean the words as a warning, but that's just what they were. And Grace was taking it to heart. Literally.

Chapter Five

It was late when Logan headed toward the house, and he was bone tired. But there was a new foal, and that made him happy. Not wanting to track barn muck all the way from the living room, he came around back and left his dirty boots outside before walking into the kitchen. It was dark, but he could see the TV on in the family room.

The next thing he knew Grace was there and had turned on the overhead recessed lighting. "Hi."

Her fresh prettiness nearly took his breath away. Adding to the effect was the fact that someone was here to greet him. After a long day of ranch work there was almost always an empty house waiting. The wave of loneliness following that thought was pretty close to pain.

"Logan?"

"Sorry. I didn't think anyone was awake."

"Cassie tried to stay up to see you but couldn't keep her eyes open. She wanted to show you her hair. She and Tracy went to the salon for a trial run."

"I'm sorry I missed it," he said.

"I took pictures for you." She slid her cell from her jeans pocket and moved close while touching the phone screen to find what she wanted. "Here is her hair. She and her mom decided part up and the rest down her back. There will be flowers at the crown where the sides are pulled on the top of her head."

She scrolled through several photos, all from different

angles, but he was having trouble concentrating because Grace smelled so damn good. And he could feel the warmth of her body, what with her arm brushing his. That sure as hell fried his brain, but he had to come up with an appropriate response or his secret would be out. The one about how badly he wanted her.

Logan cleared his throat. "Her hair looks really pretty."

"She thought so and was very excited." Grace looked up at him and smiled. "I have some shots of her dress, but she doesn't want you to see it until she walks down the aisle. Her mom told her it's a thing that the groom doesn't get to see the bride until then, so your daughter decided that worked for her, too."

"Did you get to see it?"

"Of course. It's just the men who are kept in the dark."

"So it's a rule?" he asked.

"One of the most sacred. Female code of the road— always make an entrance."

"Whatever makes her happy."

Logan was pretty sure if Grace entered a room and he was blindfolded, the scent of her skin would give her away and he'd be dazzled. For a split second he was afraid he'd said that out loud, but she wasn't looking at him with a horrified expression on her face. Maybe it would be possible to get his head on straight if he put some distance between them. He walked over to the sink and thoroughly washed his hands.

"It's late," she said. "Did you eat anything?"

"No. I'll just have a quick sandwich or something, then hit the sack."

"There aren't any leftovers from dinner. Tracy fed Cassie after shopping, before she dropped her off here. And I had a salad."

"No problem. I'll find something. Why don't you go on up to bed."

Bed. A three-letter word that made his body go tight with need. He got a vivid picture in his mind of him, her and a mattress with their bodies so close you couldn't see light between them. He wasn't sure what he'd done wrong to deserve this punishment, but without a doubt there would be a screwup in his future. Maybe he could bank this torture to pay for it.

"I'll go up. But only after you get a proper hot meal." Her voice was full of stubbornness, and he just didn't have the energy to fight her on this.

"That sounds good." Understatement of the century, he thought. It sounded too awesome to be real.

"Sit down. I'll get you a beer."

"Waiting on me is not really in your job description."

"Then let's just call it my good deed for the day," she said.

"Okay." Again he was too tired to argue and just sat on a stool at the island.

She opened the refrigerator and checked out the contents. "I'm thinking omelet. Quick, hot, satisfying."

Like sex, he thought. He was on a roll. Maybe his sister was right about men being pigs. At the very least he had a one-track mind, and this seemed to be his fallback position every time he saw Grace.

She glanced over her shoulder. "Does that sound okay to you?"

"Yeah."

She nodded, then grabbed a longneck beer and tried unsuccessfully to twist off the cap. Without a word, she handed it to him. "That is not my area of expertise," she said once he took it. "I'm better with cooking."

"I can handle it." He easily opened the bottle.

There was a wry expression on her face. "I loosened it for you."

"Keep telling yourself that."

"I plan to. Denial works for me."

That got a reluctant smile out of him. It actually made him feel better than the long drink he took from his beer.

"You should do that more often," she said.

"What? Drink?"

"No. Smile." She turned away and got busy combining mushrooms, spinach, tomatoes, cheese and eggs in a pan to cook. When the omelet was ready, she slipped it onto a plate along with a fork and slid it across to him. "Get started on that while I make some toast."

He would have told her not to go to any more trouble on his account except his mouth was full. And it tasted better than anything he'd ever eaten in his life. Could be he was starving for food. But he was pretty sure it fell more into the starving-for-*her* category.

When the bread was toasted, she buttered it and set another plate in front of him before mixing three different kinds of berries in a bowl. Finally, she fixed herself a cup of tea, then took the stool beside his and stared at his empty plate.

"I wish I could say I'm that good a cook, but you were probably hungry enough to wolf down Pop-Tarts."

"That's a fair guess. You're also a really good cook."

"I'm glad. So what kept you so late?" She cupped the steaming mug in her hands and blew on it.

The sight of her mouth made sweat bead on his forehead and had heat pooling low in his belly. Her words echoed hollowly in his head, and it took several moments to process them and form a coherent response.

"A pregnant mare went into labor. She's high risk after

having a stillborn baby, and I wanted to be there when she foaled."

"Is the baby okay?" Grace asked.

"Mother and baby are fine. Everything was textbook perfect."

"That is so cool." She smiled, and her eyes sparkled with pleasure at the news. "It's too bad Cassie didn't get to watch. She would have loved seeing the new baby horse."

"I don't know. She's kind of little to be there for that. Could be upsetting. It's not pretty." He picked up his beer and tilted the bottle toward her to make a point. "And you can call me overprotective if you want, but I can live with that."

"You're her father and have every right—no, every obligation—to question and censor what she's exposed to. And obviously Tracy should have a say. But here's something to think about. She's a rancher's kid, and animal birth is a part of that."

Even though Cassie was normally here only on weekends, Logan couldn't guarantee that a situation like this wouldn't come up during her visit. "Good point."

Grace looked thoughtful. "Although, I've never seen a horse give birth. You're probably right about her not witnessing it just yet. But I know she'll love seeing the baby."

"Yeah." He speared a strawberry with his fork. "But you also have a point. She's going to be here on the ranch, and that means being exposed to life happening on its own terms. What if I start her out with seeing the baby first? The finished product so that she knows there's a good outcome. Then maybe it wouldn't hurt for her to see kittens born or a litter of puppies."

"I think that's a wonderful idea," she said.

Her approval made him feel like a million bucks. Why did her opinion matter so much? Probably because he knew she didn't shy away from telling him when he was stepping in it, so he could believe her when she told him he was doing something right.

Could be the food hiking his blood sugar back to normal, but he wasn't as dog tired as he'd been walking up from the barn a little while ago. Or maybe his renewed energy had something to do with her company. He wasn't used to having anyone here waiting for him when he walked in the door. The fact that he liked it bothered him more than a little. But making the feeling go away was like stopping a speeding train.

He wasn't a superhero, just a man. Grace was an antidote to the loneliness he confronted every day, but his overprotective streak didn't just include Cassie. Unfortunately, he was his father's son, and sooner or later the bastard inside him would get out. His plan was to keep it from happening with Grace. He wouldn't hurt her for the world.

"Thanks for cooking." He stood and carried his dishes to the sink, then rinsed them and put everything in the dishwasher.

"Don't worry about cleaning up," she said. "I'll get the rest tomorrow."

"Okay. It's late. I'm going to get some sleep." He started to walk out of the room, then stopped to look at her. The sweetness of her pulled something tight in his chest. "Thanks again for cooking. Good night."

"You're welcome. See you tomorrow."

Not likely. Not after this sweet interlude.

"I'll be gone before you get up." And if he got back late again, she might be asleep and he could avoid her.

"Would it be all right if I bring Cassie down to the barn and you can show her the new baby horse? I'd like to see, too."

"I'll be out checking fences, but one of the hands will be around."

Something changed in her expression, as if a light just flickered and went out. As if she could read his mind and knew he was deliberately staying away from her.

"Okay, then." She walked out of the kitchen and left him standing there by himself.

The loneliness hit him like a punch to the gut. He'd disappointed her and he was truly sorry about that, but it was for her own good. He'd actually fooled himself into believing that having her here didn't have to change anything and wouldn't bother him all that much. He'd been wrong.

Now all he could do was count the days until Grace was gone and he could return to faking fatherhood on the weekends.

One second Grace had thought Logan was going to kiss her, and the next he made up an excuse not to be around to show her and Cassie the baby horse. That was two days ago, but she couldn't get it out of her mind. At least for a few hours on her afternoon off she could get out of his house.

Earlier she'd dropped Cassie off at the barn with Logan but didn't speak to him. In fact, she hadn't seen him much since that night, but there were reminders of him all over the place. In the kitchen sink, the mug he'd used for morning coffee. A stray piece of mail with his name on it. The spicy, masculine scent of him on the sofa in the family room. It was a relief to be out of there and exploring Blackwater Lake, the part locals called old town as opposed to the resort area at the foot of Black Mountain.

She parked in the lot behind Tanya's Treasures located on Main Street and used the rear entrance to go into the store. A bell signaled a walk-in for the pretty brunette who was behind the cash register counter.

Her name tag said Kelly. "Is there something I can help you find?"

"I'm looking for a wedding gift." Tracy had invited her to the nuptials because they'd hit it off, but partly to back Logan up with Cassie.

"Do you have something special in mind?"

"No, and suggestions would be really helpful. The thing is, I don't know the couple very well, so I don't want it to be too intimate, if you know what I mean."

"I think I do."

"But I want it to be really nice. Although I haven't known the bride very long, I really like her." Grace decided to stop dancing around and introduce herself. "I'm Grace Flynn."

"I know. Small town. News gets around." She shrugged. "You're taking care of Tracy and Logan's daughter, Cassie, when her mom goes on the honeymoon." The woman smiled. "I'm Kelly Black, and this is my store."

"It's nice to meet you, Kelly." Grace thought about what she'd said. "So, your middle name is Tanya?"

"No." The woman laughed. "I bought Tanya out. She met someone and moved away to be with him and get her happily-ever-after. I decided not to change the name of the store."

"You've got a lot of nice things in here, that's for sure." She looked around and noticed everything from bedside lamps dripping crystals to Blackwater Lake souvenir T-shirts.

Kelly glanced around, and her search ended up on something in the display window. "Couples go through the work and expense of a wedding for the pictures, right? What about a silver frame to put one of them in?"

"That's perfect." Grace felt like clapping her hands or hugging this woman. "Eight by ten, or five by seven?"

"Good question. I think I'd go with the smaller one. But

she can certainly return or exchange it if she'd like. And engraving of the bride's and groom's names and the date of their wedding is available. We can do it before you give it to her if you want to take a chance on the size, or she can bring it in later to have it done."

Grace thought for a moment and made up her mind. "Five by seven, and hold off on the engraving. I'll let her know that's available."

"I can take care of that with an information card inside the box with the frame. Also, if you'd like, I can do complimentary gift wrap for you."

"Yes, please."

Kelly smiled. "I wish all my customers were as easy to please as you."

"You made it easy. But I suppose difficult people are a fact of life. Every job has its drawbacks."

In Grace's case it was the complicated yet too-handsome-for-his-own-good cowboy who was her boss. Some would say she was crazy to complain about the scenery at work, but beauty was only skin-deep. Logan was more than that. There was something about him, some hard-to-define quality that pulled her in and wouldn't let go. That's not what she'd signed up for, so it was a good thing this job was temporary.

"I'll get a boxed frame from my inventory in the back, put in the printed card and take care of the wrapping. I also have gift cards for different occasions. Would you like me to include one for a wedding? It's blank, so you can fill it in."

"That would be fabulous."

While her purchase was being taken care of, Grace browsed the shelves and corners of Tanya's Treasures. She found more than one item that tempted her but held back because all her money was going into her house fund and it wouldn't be long until her dream was a reality. *Eyes on the prize*, she reminded herself.

When she left the gift shop, it was past lunchtime and starvation mode set in. Bag in hand, she walked down the street to the Harvest Café for a bite to eat. Just as she got to the door, she saw Logan's houseboat-building brother reach for the handle to open it.

"Hey, Grace." Tucker smiled. "Where's Cassie?"

"With her dad. This is my afternoon off." She held up her handled brown bag. "I've been shopping."

"That can work up an appetite." He angled his head toward the restaurant. "You're going in?"

"Yeah. Late lunch. You?"

"Same." He thought for a moment. "How do you feel about eating alone?"

"You know, when I was a little girl I always said my goal in life was to eat alone." She grinned. "Just kidding. I'm not a fan. I think it's a lot like solitary confinement."

"Let me rephrase. I don't particularly enjoy eating alone. Would you like to join me?"

"That would be nice. Thanks for asking, Tucker."

He opened the door and they walked in together. Lucy Bishop happened to be standing by the hostess stand, and there was surprise in her eyes.

"Grace, how are you? Nice to see you again. Hey, Tucker."

Was there a slight edge to her voice? Or it could just be Grace's low blood sugar inducing hallucinations of a teeny, tiny bit of jealousy. "I'm fine. I've been shopping and missed lunch. Then I ran into Tucker just outside."

"I had a meeting with clients."

"Your first Blackwater Lake houseboat contract?" When he nodded, Lucy clapped her hands, then jumped into his arms for a big hug. "Congratulations."

"Thanks."

"Look at you trying to be all nonchalant. I know inside you're doing the happy dance." Lucy playfully slugged him in the arm.

Grace studied him carefully. He appeared as relaxed and composed, as if he'd been fishing all morning. "I'm not seeing the happy dance in him."

"You have to know what you're looking for," Lucy said. "It's enough that I know it's there."

Tucker squirmed under the glare of a double whammy of female scrutiny. "Can't a hardworking man get something to eat around here?"

"Hey, shopping works up an appetite, too," Grace protested.

"Truer words were never spoken," Lucy agreed. "Let's get some food into you quick."

"Really?" Tucker said, looking from one to the other. "Shopping takes priority over an exclusive houseboat community on Blackwater Lake?"

"See? I knew he was high-fiving himself." Lucy grinned and looked around. There were only a few diners in the place. "So pick a table, any table."

"Don't have to ask me twice." Tucker headed for one by the window that looked out on Main Street.

Grace followed and took the seat across from him.

"Do you need a menu, Grace? Twenty bucks says that Tucker will order the chicken salad croissant with coleslaw and fruit."

He opened his mouth but seemed to think better of what he planned to say. "That sounds good."

"Make it two."

"Coming right up," Lucy said.

Grace saw the woman glance at Tucker one last time before moving away. She remembered Lucy saying that someone should marry this man, then swearing up and down that that someone would not be her. Not that she was an expert, but it sure looked like they had chemistry. Hmm.

"So," Tucker said, drawing her gaze back to him. "You already know how my work is going. What's up with you?"

"Your niece is a perfect angel. I love taking care of her. *She* makes my job not even a job."

He met her gaze. "I couldn't help hearing a slight emphasis on *she*. Does that mean Logan is making things tough?"

"He loves his daughter very much." Did dumping on your boss's brother count as biting the hand that feeds you?

"Loving her that way can present different kinds of challenges."

"That's very insightful of you. Do you have kids?" she asked.

"Not yet. But I'd like to very much."

Men didn't usually admit to being in touch with their feminine side so readily. It made her wonder. "What's stopping you?"

"I haven't met the right woman." He shrugged.

"There's no one from your past you made a pact with that if you're both thirty and haven't met 'the one,' you'll have a child together?"

"No." He laughed. "But back to my brother. Logan is giving you a hard time?"

"Not at all. He's a good man. It's just that I worry…"

"About?"

"He seems to hold back with Cassie. His kid instincts are great, but he doesn't trust them." She saw something flicker in the man's gaze and took a guess about what it might be. "Logan told me about your mom leaving your dad and having no place to go."

"Oh." Tucker nodded slowly, as if he'd been weighing how much to say. "It was hard on all of us, but particularly Logan because he's the oldest. Mom relied on him to take care of us when she was working. He was the one we looked to. When we were hungry he scavenged through Dumpsters for perfectly good thrown-away food. He took us into public restrooms and supervised us washing up. He got us to school and made sure strangers left us alone."

"I can't even imagine." Grace had grown up in foster care and went from home to home, which was tough, but she always had a roof over her head. It was someone else's roof, but still… Nothing like what Logan and his siblings went through.

"Then my grandfather took us in. He was a good man and taught us boys how to be good men. But he was alone because my grandmother left him. And my mom married a man who couldn't be a worse husband or father."

"At least you and your siblings were all together," she said.

"True, and we were grateful for that. But neither side of our family was a shining example of a healthy relationship. It had an impact on all of us. Especially Logan, I think. And he takes the responsibility of raising and protecting Cassie to heart. Bottom line is we have no template of what love and family should look like."

He wasn't the only one, Grace thought. She was right there in that boat with Logan. Maybe something to bond over? But he walked away from kissing her. It was about not wanting to compromise her but still…

That was awfully noble really and tugged at her soft mushy center that he put her in the category of people to be protected. But she didn't need him to do that. Clearly she and Logan were two lost souls who couldn't let themselves take a chance on forever.

She was also a product of her environment. She lost count of which placement it was when she'd made an instinctive decision not to let herself care because the foster family was temporary. The only time she'd let a man in, he took advantage of her. But property was permanent.

That's why her dream was to buy a house. A girl could count on four walls and a roof. It wouldn't break her heart.

Only a man could do that, and she wouldn't give him the chance.

Chapter Six

Logan missed Grace on her afternoon off, and it was more than just the fact that he liked being around her. Too much, really. When he took care of Cassie, work came to a halt. Ranch chores had to wait so he could focus only on her. But his little girl was getting bored. Normally on the weekend they shopped or went to a movie, but today was just a couple of hours and those things weren't practical.

Right now she was watching a DVD of an animated mermaid movie and hanging off the side of the family room sofa. He'd seen her riveted by things on TV, but this wasn't one of those times.

"Daddy, I wanna go see the baby horse."

God, he hated when he was right.

"A baby horse is a foal," he corrected. "And you just saw him a little while ago."

"But I wanna see him again. And he needs a name, Daddy. We can't just keep sayin' 'him.'"

He sat down on the sofa beside her. "So let's talk about names. Give me some ideas."

Switching her position, she was lying on the seat cushion with her legs up in the air and resting on the sofa back. "I hafta see him again. To make sure it's the very rightest name for him."

If she would stand still and just look he'd have no problem, but that never happened. She moved so fast and had a bad habit of disappearing. In the barn there were so many corners where he couldn't see her, not to mention tools and sharp things she shouldn't touch but always wanted to. She was safe right here in the house. He could live with her being bored until Grace got back. Which should be soon. It was almost dinnertime, and she'd told him to expect her before then.

"The horse is probably sleeping. That's when he grows."

"I won't wake him up," she promised. "I can be really quiet. Please, Daddy."

It was the pleading expression in her big eyes that got to him. That and hearing Grace's voice in his head saying that she's a rancher's kid.

"Okay, but you have to stay right next to me," he warned.

"I will."

"No running wild. There are things in the barn that can hurt you, Cassie. We're just going to look at the baby."

"Foal," she said, grinning.

"Right."

"And I get to name him."

"Okay. Let's go." He got up from the sofa and turned off the movie before the two of them went outside, then headed to the right toward the corral. She started to run and he said, "Cass, what did I just tell you?"

She gave him the stink eye. "We're not at the barn yet."

That was technically true but splitting hairs anyway. In her little pink shorts, her bare legs were unprotected. "How about if we just walk so you don't fall down and get hurt? Your mom is getting married the day after tomorrow. You don't want to ruin the effect of that pretty flower girl dress with a skinned knee, right?"

"I guess so."

"Good." Because that's how it was going to be on his watch. He held out his hand, and in spite of the pout on her pretty little face, she took it.

The sun was lowering in the sky, and again he wondered when Grace would get back. It seemed an eternity since she'd brought Cassie to him in the barn then immediately left for the afternoon. He couldn't look at her hard enough for those few minutes, and he wanted to kiss her. The only way he knew to prevent that was to maintain his distance. But that didn't keep him from missing her.

They walked into the barn, where the new mother and baby were safe and secure in the first stall.

"Look, Daddy, he's awake."

"I see that."

Cassie peeked through the slats as the little guy came over to her on his spindly legs. She held out her hand and touched him. "Hi, boy. I can't see him very well," she complained.

"I'll lift you up."

"But then I won't be able to touch him."

Catch-22, and it called for a distraction. The mare provided it when she moved closer to keep a watchful eye on her baby. Logan sure understood that.

"Have you come up with any names yet?" he asked his daughter.

"I was thinkin' about Olaf or Kristoff."

Logan had watched all the animated movies and knew those two were characters from *Frozen*. He'd promised she could name the foal and would keep his word. But... Olaf? Fortunately, this little guy wouldn't have to beat up any kids at school who made fun of his name.

"Do you have any other ideas?" Please, God.

"Gus Gus, maybe."

That was one of the mice from *Cinderella*. So he could see where she was going with this. It was marginally better. "What else?"

"How about Gaston or Prince Charming?" She looked up at him hopefully.

It was a darn shame she was too young for grown-up movies because he could get behind more manly names like Braveheart, Black Jack or Rambo. "Prince Charming isn't bad."

She climbed up on the second slat of the fence and he was about to say something, but she stopped there. "It's not the rightest one."

"What else have you got?"

"Well, he has dark hair like Prince Eric from *The Little Mermaid*."

Logan could live with that. "Not bad."

"Really?" She had moved up another slat, getting closer to eye to eye with him.

"What do you think?"

"Eric." She was testing it out loud again. "I like it."

"Me, too. Eric it is."

Logan thought he heard a car, and his pulse jumped. It could be Grace. He moved several steps to the open barn door and looked up toward the house. There was no sign of her, and the way his heart fell was pretty amazing—and not in a good way. He shouldn't feel anything but neutral, but that wasn't the case. Obviously, it was personal.

"Daddy, look at me!"

He turned and saw his daughter had climbed to the top of the stall's gate. And she wasn't holding on. Her hands were up in the air.

"Cassie—" The sharp tone in his voice startled her, and she fell.

It seemed to happen in slow motion, and just like a nightmare, he couldn't get there in time to catch her. She cried out and landed on both knees. For a split second she made no sound at all, then the crying started.

"Daddy—"

He rushed over and scooped her up, noting the blood on her legs. "I've got you, baby girl."

Tears were streaming down her face, and her little chest was heaving from the sobs. He carried her out of the barn and up to the house. In the downstairs bathroom, he set her on the counter in order to assess the damage. Both knees were scraped and had bits of dirt and hay in them. He had never wished for Grace to be there as much as he did at that moment. More than anything he wanted to turn first aid over to her.

But this couldn't wait, and he was the last line of defense. "I have to clean up these scrapes, baby girl."

"No, Daddy. It will sting."

"If I don't it will hurt worse, honey."

"Don't. Please, Daddy." Tears had made muddy tracks through the dirt on her face.

If he said it was going to hurt him more than her there was no way she'd understand, but that didn't make it any less true. "How about this. If I hurt you cleaning this up, you can punch me in the arm five times."

That got her attention. "Ten times."

"Can you count that high?"

"Grace taught me to count to fifty. Maybe even higher." She was a tough negotiator.

"Do you want to hit me as many times as you can count?" He was willing if that would make her feel better.

"No. But maybe up to twenty."

"You drive a hard bargain." He pretended to think it over. "Deal."

She made a fist and held it out for a bump from him to seal the bargain. He obliged.

"Okay. I'm going to swing your legs over the sink and turn on the water." He'd heard Grace talk to Cassie and explain what was going to happen. Now seemed like a good time to do that. "I'll squirt a little hand soap on—"

"Don't rub it," she cried out.

"I won't. Then I'll scoop water on to wash off the soap. When it's all clean I'll put peroxide—"

"What's that?"

He got out the brown bottle, antibiotic ointment and bandages from the medicine cabinet. "It's this. It looks like water."

"Will it sting?"

He couldn't lie to her. "It might a little. But it will bubble up."

Her eyes grew wide. "My boo-boo blows bubbles?"

"Yeah. Kind of. To kill germs so it won't get infected. When that dries we'll put on some cream to kill germs, then bandages."

"The Ariel ones?"

"Yup. Do you want to hold them?"

"Okay."

"You ready to do this?" When she nodded, he took a deep breath and did exactly what he'd said. Bits of hay and dirt along with soap went down the drain. He finished off with the peroxide while she was busy unwrapping the bandages. She hadn't made a peep.

"Look, Daddy, there's the bubbles."

"Told you. Now we have to wait for this to dry or the bandages won't stick. But the worst is over."

"Do I get to punch your arm now?" She looked unsure about that.

"Did it hurt?"

"No."

"Well, you can if you want to," he said.

"That's okay. I don't want to hurt you."

It would make him feel better. He deserved worse for letting this happen.

"Daddy!" That was her crisis-in-progress tone.

"What's wrong? Where do you hurt?" He put his palm on her abdomen. It wasn't possible she had internal injuries, was it?

"I'm going to have skinned-up knees when Mommy gets married and it will ruin my pretty dress just like you said."

And the hits just keep on coming, he thought. What was he going to tell her now? He thought for a moment. "Didn't you tell me your dress goes almost to your ankles?"

She nodded and handed over the unwrapped bandages. "Like Belle's yellow dress."

"Then it will cover your boo-boos. They will not show when you walk down the aisle at your mom's wedding."

"You sure?"

"As much as I can be since you won't let me see it until the big day," he said.

The little girl looked past him and smiled. "Grace! Do you think my dress will cover my boo-boos like Daddy said?"

"Absolutely it will."

Cassie's smile was radiant. "Can we put the bandages on now?"

"Sure." He looked in the mirror and met Grace's gaze. "Do you want to do the honors?"

"Nope." She folded her arms over her chest.

He sighed and put on the ointment before finishing off with the protective covering. "You're good to go."

The little girl threw her arms around his neck. "Thank you, Daddy."

"You're welcome." He lifted her down.

"I'm going to get the picture I made for Grace." Then she was gone.

Logan rubbed a hand across his neck. "How long were you standing there?"

"From when you agreed to take twenty slugs for team Cassie."

"Okay, let me have it. I was wrong how many ways?" Before she could say anything, he continued, "She climbed on the gate to look at Eric—"

"Who?"

"That's what she named the foal. I just took my eyes off her for a minute." *To look for you*, he thought, but didn't say that. "It happened so fast."

"Don't beat yourself up, Logan. She's a kid and stuff happens. It's literally impossible to watch them every single second. And look at it this way. Cheap lesson. She'll be more careful the next time she climbs on anything. The scrapes will heal, and as you pointed out, they will not show when she wears her dress."

"The words are all nice, but I know you're judging."

She made a scoffing sound. "Actually, I was thinking that you should give lessons on first aid for five-year-olds."

He shrugged. "Just doing what had to be done."

"That's what a good dad does. And you get an A-plus in daddying. You should know I grade tough, so that means a lot."

"You teach kindergarten," he said wryly.

"Still, in my class every grade is earned." She patted him on the back. "Nice job, Logan."

"Thanks."

"I'll get dinner started. It's just hamburgers and hot dogs."

"Sounds good."

She nodded, then backed out of the room and left him alone. Imagine that. Mary Poppins gave him a passing grade. He felt pretty damn pleased about that. Her good opinion meant a lot to him. Later he would worry about how bad that was, but right now he didn't have the energy to question the reaction.

And she'd touched him. That pleased him, too, but the memory of that touch was going to keep him awake tonight.

Grace put the finishing touches on her makeup, going with a dramatic smoky eye for Tracy's evening wedding. She'd bought some new shadow, eyeliner and mascara on her day off and had experimented. The results were worth it, she thought, studying her reflection in the bathroom mirror. But the rollers the size of Coke cans had to go. And they did.

The hair and makeup gods were on her side today because she brushed out the shiny strands that fell past her shoulders and assessed the results. Full but not too curvy, no further fussing necessary.

Now for her dress. She'd brought one with her from Buckskin Pass because Tracy had made it clear she wanted Grace at the wedding to help with Cassie. The floral, crepe, sleeveless number had a matching belt and fit her curves like someone had her shape in mind when making it. Something fun and maybe the tiniest bit sexy. Not that she planned to take the sex part out for a spin. This was part of her job, but a girl still wanted to look good.

She took the plastic covering off the dress and lifted it from the hanger, then stepped into it. After pulling the material up over her hips, she slid her arms in and reached behind to do the zipper.

Then she remembered. This dress had required zipper assistance from the saleswoman. It was tight and her arms weren't long enough, nor did they bend the right way to get that little tab where it was supposed to be in order to not flash skin.

She bought the thing because she fell in love with the look and fit, figuring her landlady, Janice Erwin, would give her a hand if necessary. This was something Cassie could handle, but she wasn't here. The little girl had spent the night with her mom and they were getting ready together.

This was a major problem. She wasn't sure whether or not Logan was still in the house. He hadn't shared his wedding-day itinerary with her. Since Cassie was squared away, he had no reason to speak to Grace at all and hadn't much, not since grading his first-aid skills. And before that the night she'd thought he was going to kiss her. After she fixed him dinner.

The way to a man's heart being through his stomach was a flawed saying. Not that she wanted any man's heart. Bottom line: there was no one here to help with her darn zipper.

She could think of only one thing to do. She had a shawl, pink to pick up one of the shades in the material, and would just have to wear it until she could grab a woman to help.

She looked at herself in the full-length, freestanding mirror in her room as she buckled the belt. Then she pivoted to glance at the back where the sides of her dress gapped. "It's not technically a wardrobe malfunction so much as a glitch right out of the starting gate."

It was early, but she would just head over to Holden House, where the wedding and reception were being held. The bride and her attendants were already there, so someone could fix her up, then she might be of some use to Tracy.

She slipped on her four-inch pink pumps, grabbed her purse and wrap and headed down the stairs. When she got to the bottom, she heard one of the steps behind her squeak. The loose tread meant she wasn't alone after all.

And her dress wasn't zipped. She whirled around and

backed up against the wall, then met Logan's gaze as he took the last two steps. "Hi. I didn't think you were still here."

"My presence isn't required until later. The photographer is getting photos of the bride, groom and the wedding party, so lucky for you, I haven't left yet."

She blinked up at him. He was close enough to feel the heat of his body and his breath on her face. "L-lucky?"

"It looks like you could use some help with your dress."

The darkly intense expression on his face made her wonder if he was offering to zip the dress or take it off. Quite frankly, right that second she hoped it was the latter. Then rational thought returned.

"Help? Right. The zipper. That's okay. I'll find someone when I get there."

"Don't be silly." He made a circle with his finger, indicating she should turn around. "Two seconds and you're decent."

"I'm hardly indecent now. More of me is covered by this half-closed dress than the average woman in a bikini."

It didn't seem possible but his eyes actually went a shade darker, and her pulse started to race. But he was right that she was making a big deal out of nothing. Two seconds and she would be out of here and on her way. She'd see him again at the wedding, but a lot of people were attending and he could go back to ignoring her again.

Without another word she turned, giving him access to the back of the dress. It must have been her imagination, his small intake of breath, but his hesitation was enough to make her glance over her shoulder.

"Is there a problem? Is the zipper caught?"

"No." The word was like a growl—gruff and hoarse. He cleared his throat and pulled the zipper up, then secured it with the hook and eye at the top.

Obviously, the man knew his way around a woman's clothes, but probably from removing them, not making sure they stayed on.

And don't even get her started on the touch of his fingers on her neck. Tingles tap-danced down her arms, and that was bad. If ever she needed not to be distracted, it was now.

She faced him again. "Thank you."

"Don't mention it." He looked her up and down, his gaze stopping the longest on her pink heels. "You look nice."

"Thanks."

"Just stating a fact."

She thought her glam squad—namely herself—had outdone itself. So hats off for making her look awesome. And then for the first time she noticed him and almost said wow.

"You look nice, too." Just to be a smart-ass, she let her gaze wander over him just like he'd done to her. "Just stating a fact."

Logan was wearing a traditional black tuxedo with a crisp white shirt and bow tie. He personified the word *awesome* and took her breath away for the second time in the last two minutes. In his cowboy gear of jeans, snap-front shirt, scuffed boots and worn Stetson, he would have women throwing their phone numbers at him like confetti.

But this dashing, elegant look revealed a side to him that was positively heart-stopping. The black jacket fit him perfectly, outlining his broad shoulders, and made her want to run her palms over the width of them. His brown hair was recently trimmed and combed, although the tendency to curl couldn't be completely tamed. No doubt like the man himself.

It was a darn good thing a lot of people would be there tonight to blunt the force of what this man did to her. She wasn't prone to quivering inside, and the only way to make it stop was to get the heck away from him.

"Well, thanks again, Logan. I better get going. See if I can do anything to help Tracy."

"I'm heading out, too. Told her I'd be there early just in case."

"Right. So, I guess I'll see you there." She took a step to the side, intending to walk past him.

"Hold on." He put his fingers on her arm, but it was probably an automatic gesture, judging by the surprised look that jumped into his eyes. And the speed with which he dropped his hand.

"What?" she asked.

"We should ride over together."

"To the wedding," she clarified, not sure if she'd heard him right.

The corners of his mouth curved up as he glanced down at his tuxedo pants and shiny shoes. "I think we're over-dressed for a rodeo."

"No—I meant—" She couldn't help laughing. This was the old Logan, the one who was friendly and funny, before he wasn't. He'd been successfully keeping his distance from her, so his voluntarily suggesting being in the same vehicle had come as something of a surprise. "You don't want to be stuck with me if there's something you have to do."

"I doubt that will happen. And being *stuck* with you isn't exactly what I'd call it."

"Oh? What would you call it?" She couldn't help asking, then literally held her breath while waiting for an answer.

"Carpooling."

"Right." She nodded. "Because saving gas is always a good thing."

He grinned. "You in?"

So much more than she should be. "Yes."

"My truck is parked out front, by the porch. I'll drive."

"Okay."

Grace followed him outside and saw the bright red pickup where he said it would be. Side by side they walked down the steps, with her treading carefully in her very high heels. He opened the door for her, and then she saw a logistical issue. This truck didn't have a running board. With her very tight skirt there was no way she could climb into the cab of this vehicle without sacrificing her dignity.

Chapter Seven

"I have a problem." Grace looked up at Logan. "There's no way for me to get from down here to up there in any sort of ladylike way. Maybe we should take my car?"

"No way I'm riding in that dinky thing. Hold on." The warning was barely out of his mouth before he scooped her up and set her on the truck's passenger seat. "Problem solved."

Be still my heart, she thought. She wondered what Logan Hunt would do if she batted her eyelashes and said, "You're so manly and strong." The intrepid cowboy would probably run for his life, and the idea of hitting him with a full-on, in-your-face flirt made her smile.

But all she said was, "Thanks."

"You're welcome." He shut the door and walked around to the driver's side and easily climbed in.

Grace glowed from head to toe and marveled that his fleeting touch could do that and rocked it all the way to Holden House. It was just starting to fade when he parked the truck then came around to the passenger side. She'd opened the door, intending to use gravity this time and just slide down. But he settled his hands at her waist and lifted her to the ground. How often did she get a courtly gesture from a handsome man? Um… Never in her world.

"Thanks for the ride, Logan. I guess I'll see you at the wedding."

"Where are you going?"

"To see if Tracy or Cassie needs anything. Your daughter might be getting restless with all the standing around."

He nodded. "I'll go check on the groom. See you later."

Grace found the suite where the bride and her attendants were getting ready and was instantly swept up in the excitement. She zipped, fetched and fluffed whatever needed fluffing. Then Hadley Michaels, the hotel events coordinator, arrived. That was their signal for go time, so Grace slipped out and headed for the wedding venue downstairs.

Chairs were set up in one of the conference rooms, and the reception would immediately follow in the room beside it. At the door she was greeted by one of the groomsmen. Tracy had instructed her to tell him that she was to sit in the first row, in case Cassie got fidgety standing for the vows. He bypassed the aisle and took her around to her predetermined place. The room was filled with flowers—roses, star lilies and baby's breath—and it smelled like a garden. Dark wood trim, a crystal chandelier and wall sconces gave the scene the feel of country elegance. Off to the side a string quartet played soothing background music. As people arrived, she heard a low hum of voices behind her.

Then everyone went silent and the music changed to the traditional wedding march. Along with the other guests, Grace stood, then inched to the end of her row and was in place just as the double doors at the back of the room opened. One by one the attendants in their strapless, chiffon blush-pink dresses slowly moved toward her. Behind them she saw Cassie, in her princess-length white dress with the embroidered rosebuds and pink satin bow. She walked down the aisle dropping rose petals as if she did it every day.

The little girl grinned at Grace as she passed, then took her place with the other bridesmaids. When they were in position, the beautiful bride appeared in the doorway in her white strapless, full-skirted gown. But what put a lump the size of Montana in Grace's throat was Logan walking the mother of his child down the aisle. It was a sign of their sweet, strong friendship and brought tears to her eyes.

As the two passed her, she caught a whiff of his spicy scent, then he was placing Tracy's hand into her groom's. Just when it didn't seem possible he could be any sweeter, Logan went all protective.

His voice was muted, but the words were audible to anyone in the front row. "You better take care of her. And I'm not kidding."

Grace didn't have a tissue in her purse, so she used the edge of her shawl to dab at her eyes. After issuing his warning, Logan backed away from the bride and groom and took his place in the reserved chair beside hers.

He looked down and frowned. "Why are you crying?"

"It's a wedding," she whispered. "Women cry. And I didn't know you were giving Tracy away."

He shrugged. "She asked."

"It's very sweet."

Then the minister instructed everyone to sit down for the ceremony. There were religious readings, poems and vows the couple had written to each other. Cassie did get restless, so Grace motioned her over and the little girl sat between her and Logan. Grace's heart squeezed tight. For just a moment she knew what it felt like to be part of a family. That had never happened to her before. It was lovely. But belonging somewhere was a dream she'd lost hope of ever having, so she pushed the feeling away and concentrated on this wedding.

The bride and groom repeated promises to love, honor and respect each other, exchanged rings and shared their first kiss as husband and wife. Afterward they walked back down the aisle followed by everyone in the wedding party, including Logan and Cassie. Guests filed into the next room, which was set up for dinner and dancing. Grace waited in the receiving line to offer congratulations to the new couple.

Tracy gave her a hug. "Thank you for being there. Everything went so smoothly with Cassie."

"I appreciate your including me. It was perfect," Grace assured her.

"This is my—" Tracy smiled at the dark-haired man beside her. "I've gotten so used to saying fiancé. This is my *husband*, Denver Graham."

"That would make you Mrs. Graham." The love in her groom's eyes was palpable when he looked at her. Then he smiled at Grace. "Thanks for being here."

"Congratulations."

She moved away and saw that the majority of guests were sitting down, so she found her seat at the table where Logan and his siblings were.

"Hello," Tucker said.

"Hey." She smiled at him. "Nice to see you again."

"Again?" Logan's gaze narrowed.

"We had lunch together," his brother explained.

"Is there something we should know?" Jamie Hart was sitting across from her.

"No. It was my afternoon off and I was shopping. So I missed lunch that day and ran into Tucker at the Harvest Café. We decided to keep each other company."

"It was a nice surprise," Tucker said. "I usually eat alone."

"You might want to think about why that is." Logan was scowling at him.

"I was buying a wedding gift, actually." Grace wasn't sure what was bugging him but decided this might be a good time for a distraction. "It seemed appropriate to do that even though Tracy mostly wanted me here to help with Cassie."

Max was sitting beside her. "So you really are here in a working capacity?"

She looked around at the flowers, elegant china, crystal chandeliers and people dressed up—some in tuxedos. She sneaked a glance at Logan sitting on her other side. "If you can call this working."

"Don't you ever give Grace a night off?" Jamie shot her brother a teasing look.

"Everything is in her contract," he defended.

"He's right," she said. "I knew what I was signing up for." Although it hadn't been spelled out that he would literally sweep her off her feet and make her heart go pitter-pat. "I don't mind. And I wouldn't have missed seeing Cassie in her flower girl dress for anything. It's a good thing I had an invitation or I'd have been forced to crash the wedding."

"No crashing necessary," Max said. "I'd be happy to have you as my plus one."

She glanced at each of them, all single. "Now that you mention it, not one of you is here with a date. What's up with that?" The four of them stared wordlessly at each other as if she'd asked them the secret to world peace. "Seriously. The four of you are fun and better-than-average-looking. You can't tell me that no one in this town would go out with you."

"I don't know what's wrong with the rest of them," Max finally said, "but I chose to come alone so as not to be distracted from the celebration of love we're here to take part in."

"You are so full of it. If I was sitting closer, I'd punch you." With all those muscles, he probably wouldn't even feel it. Jamie's face took on a wicked expression. "What's really going on is that the word is out. Hockey players don't make very good lovers."

"Now who's full of it?" Max's teasing facade slipped a little. "And I'm retired from hockey."

"What about you, Tucker?" Grace remembered him saying he wanted children. Coming stag to a wedding wasn't helping his cause.

"I've been busy," he said vaguely.

"He's got no game," Logan joked.

"That is classic pot calling the kettle black," his brother shot back. "What's your excuse for coming alone?"

"I didn't. I came with Grace." Logan grinned at all of them.

That was literally true, but it wasn't technically a date. She gave him a wry look. "Does carpooling count?"

That produced a rash of ribbing from the three Harts, but Logan gave as good as he got. These four were pros at this back-and-forth thing. It was good-natured and based on a shared history of hardship, loyalty and love.

Even when there was nothing they'd had everything because they were together. Watching them made her think about growing up in foster care. No one was mean or abusive to her, but there was no teasing banter, just polite acceptance. Like a duty. She was always on the outside looking in, never quite a part of the family unit. Apparently carpooling with Logan was a metaphor for her life, just going along for the ride. Maybe it was time to be proactive.

Conversation and joking continued as dinner was served and wine poured. Everyone relaxed and had a good time. Except for having the father of her child give her away, Tracy had opted for traditional in all the decisions. Throwing the bouquet and garter, not to mention the chicken dance. Those pictures were going to be hilarious.

Because this was an evening wedding, it would go on

past Cassie's bedtime. During the festivities, Grace kept a watchful eye on the little girl, looking for the classic signs that she was overtired and ready to melt down. She'd wandered over and climbed into the sixth chair at their table. Her aunt and uncles had kept her busy talking and admiring her pretty dress. When the server was distributing wedding cake, there wasn't a single piece on his tray with a flower and he tried to give one of the boring ones to Cassie. The tears started flowing.

All three men were ready to go track down an icing flower, but Grace stopped them with a look. She got up and circled the table, then picked up the little girl before settling her on her lap. "I'm sorry you didn't get the cake you wanted, sweetie."

"But the flowers are the best." Her small body shook with sobs that had nothing to do with cake and everything to do with being overtired.

"I know. But it's getting late, little one. How about we get you home to bed?" Grace was prepared for push back, but it didn't come.

Cassie yawned and curled in a little closer. "Okay. Can we, Daddy?"

"Ready when you are, baby girl." He pushed his chair back, preparing to stand.

"I'll gather up her things," Grace said, "and then we'll—"

"Hey, Cass," Jamie interrupted. "How about coming home with me? We haven't had a sleepover in a long time."

"Can I sleep in your pretty bed, Aunt Jamie?"

"Of course. I wouldn't have it any other way. And you can wear my lacy nightgown. We'll play princess."

"Awesome." The child had an energy spurt and jumped off Grace's lap, then ran to her aunt.

"You don't have to do that, Jamie," Logan protested. "You should stay and have fun."

She put her arm around her niece. "I've had enough happily-ever-after for one day. It's making my teeth hurt. Grace should get a night off. You two stay and have fun. I won't take no for an answer. It's settled. I'll just let Tracy know what's going on."

Cassie's care for the night might be settled, but Grace was not. It wasn't at all clear what it meant for the two of them to stay and have fun. But if it felt anything like him scooping her into his arms earlier, this scenario had the potential to make her positively giddy. And she wasn't entirely sure whether or not that was fear or anticipation talking.

There were only a few stragglers left at the reception now, just the hard-core party crowd. Logan wasn't normally one of them, but tonight was different. He'd been with Grace, and time flew by. He hadn't had so much fun in a very long time and didn't want to leave, even though his feet hurt from dancing and his jaw from laughing. He hadn't done that in a long time either.

Logan set a glass of white wine down on the table in front of Grace. He'd volunteered to get her one when the last-call notice was given. She thanked him, then took a sip of the golden liquid.

"Things are winding down," he said, sitting beside her.

"Yeah. I'm getting that feeling."

"I think the bride and groom want to go to bed."

She had another drink, then set the long-stemmed glass on the white tablecloth. "Well, of course they do. They just got married."

"Yeah."

"I wonder where they're spending their wedding night."

"Here at Holden House. In the bridal suite."

Grace put her elbow on the table and rested her chin in her palm. "And you know their intimate plans...how?"

There was intimate and then there was *intimate*. It was a no-brainer they would be having sex, what with their taking vows that made them husband and wife. The location of that sex he knew for another reason. "Renting the bridal suite for their wedding night was my gift to them."

"That's really sweet." She smiled at him a little tipsily. "I just got them a silver photo frame."

"And very thoughtful of you to do that."

"Yours is better." She looked at him for a moment, then took another sip of wine. "They only have to go up in the elevator to do the wild thing."

He really wished she would talk about flowers, rocks or the weather and quit mentioning sex. Tracy's new husband would get lucky tonight, but Logan would not. All evening there had been long chunks of time when he forgot he was paying this woman to care for his daughter. As badly as he wanted Grace, he couldn't afford to overlook the fact that he signed her paycheck.

"Finish your drink, Cinderella."

"I thought I was Mary Poppins."

"Not tonight. It's past midnight, and the pumpkin is waiting."

She had one swallow left in the glass and did as instructed. After standing, she picked up her purse and pink wrap. "We need to say goodbye to the happy couple."

"Okay."

The music stopped and the DJ said good-night after wishing the bride and groom congratulations one last time. They walked onto the dance floor and up to Tracy and her husband, who had finished the last dance but still had their arms around each other.

The bride smiled. "Logan, I can't thank you enough for giving me away today."

"I'm glad you're happy, Trace. Hope you really didn't mind that Cassie went home with my sister."

"Not at all. She was very excited to spend the night with her aunt."

Logan held out his hand to her groom. "Congratulations, you've got yourself a great girl. Don't blow it."

Denver laughed. "There were a lot of witnesses when I promised to love, honor—and yes—obey. An easy vow to make. She's the best thing that ever happened to me."

Grace shook his hand and hugged Tracy. "I'm sure you'll be very happy. Have a wonderful honeymoon trip. I will take very good care of your daughter."

"I know. Thanks." The bride stifled a yawn. "Sorry. It's not the company. Just been a long, stressful, yet joyous day."

"And we have an early flight tomorrow," her husband reminded her.

"That's code for, 'Please, can we go now?'" Logan grinned at the other man before glancing around the room. "Do you need any help here?"

"No. The hotel will clean up, and my bridesmaids are loading up the gifts to keep for us. I know this is really late for you, Logan. I'm going to take that as a sign that you had a good time." Tracy glanced at Grace, and a speculative twinkle slipped into her eyes. As if she knew why he'd had a good time.

The woman knew him pretty well and had probably figured out how he was feeling about Grace. Time to go before she decided to share her insight.

"Okay, then. Have a great trip. Don't worry about Cassie. Good night."

There was a tender look on Tracy's face when she said, "It's you I worry about."

"No need. I'm good."

She looked at Grace, then kissed his cheek. "Not yet, you're not. But I have hope."

At least one of them did, he thought, walking out of the banquet room with Grace beside him. Lately he was having a devil of a time keeping his inner demons under control. It was anyone's guess whether or not he even deserved hope.

The truck was in the lot where he'd left it under one of the lights in the parking lot. He hit the button on his key fob to unlock the doors, then opened the passenger side. Looking down at Grace, he mumbled a curse. Whatever had possessed him to offer her a ride? The problem of her tight dress and climbing into his truck hadn't changed. Picking her up was the only solution, but it wasn't so simple this time.

After dancing with her tonight, he knew how good she felt in his arms. How perfectly she fit against him. This must be what hell felt like, he thought, as the flames of temptation licked through him.

"What's wrong, Logan? You're looking awfully intense about something."

"Nothing. It's just— I have to pick you up again," he said through gritted teeth.

"Or, you could turn your back and I'll hike my skirt up to my waist and climb in."

"Oh, for Pete's sake—" This would be quick.

He bent and lifted her but wasn't fully prepared when she slid her arms around his neck. He knew what a "come-hither" expression looked like and had even experienced it more times than he could count. But he'd never felt the power of it before Grace. He didn't think she even realized how she was looking at him. As if she wanted him, too.

This was big trouble.

It would be so easy to touch his mouth to hers. Only a couple of inches separated them, and he ached to know if she tasted of wine, cake and some magic that was all her. Somewhere close by he heard the chirp of an unlocking car. The sound snapped him out of the sensual trance, and he moved over to the truck, setting her gently in the passenger seat. It was just a beat too long before she stopped touching him.

"Thanks."

"Buckle up."

He closed the door and realized how stupid he sounded. She wasn't a kid but a grown woman, a fact not lost on him after holding her exceptional curves in his arms.

After removing his tuxedo jacket, he yanked open the driver's door and tossed the coat in the back seat. The night didn't do nearly enough to cool his heated skin. What he really needed was an ice-cold shower. And he'd take one. Fifteen minutes, twenty tops, and he would be home free. No pun intended. After sliding the key into the ignition, he turned it and the engine roared to life.

"It was a beautiful wedding, wasn't it?" Grace's voice was dreamy, and she sounded a little bit buzzed.

"I suppose."

"You don't think it was?"

"Doesn't matter what I think as long as Tracy was happy with the way it turned out."

"She looked beyond happy," Grace gushed. "And how very modern family and enlightened of you to walk her down the aisle and give her away. Especially after you once proposed to her."

It felt like a million years since he'd asked her to marry him and she'd laughed. "She told you about that?"

"Yes. But she said the two of you were much better off as friends."

"She's a smart woman." Logan knew he would have made her miserable, and that went for anyone who was foolish enough to take him on. "She waited for the right guy, and he'll be good to her."

"Because you threatened him." Grace laughed.

The sweet, happy sound unlocked empty places inside him that were off-limits. "That wasn't a threat. More of a promise."

"You're so macho and protective. I have to say it's very sexy."

No, she really didn't have to say that. The words were like throwing kerosene on the fire already burning inside him. Logan went tight with need, and he regretted giving her that last glass of wine. It had really loosened her up, and his willpower was melting like a pat of butter in a hot skillet.

He decided to change the subject. "Sure do hope we get some rain soon, otherwise wildfires could be a problem. Last summer there was a real bad one. A lot of people had to evacuate their homes. Some of them, the properties, were completely destroyed."

He was rambling, about fire of all things. It was stupid when he was already hot enough to set off dry brush with just a look. But that was better than letting her get in another comment with the word *sexy* in it.

After what felt like the longest ride of his entire life, Logan finally pulled up to his ranch house and parked. It had been only a few hours since they left here, and yet it felt like forever, too. A lifetime since he'd followed her down the stairs unable to take his eyes off her back, bare except for a bra strap.

Raising her zipper without letting his feelings show had taken a lot of self-control, and he was going to need an injection of it now as he never had before. He'd wanted her more than his next breath earlier, but he wanted her even more than that right this minute.

He blew out a long breath before exiting the truck and closing the door. Then he walked around to help her down. When he saw that she'd already slid to the ground, he felt as if he'd finally caught a break. Thank God he didn't have to touch her again.

Side by side they walked up the front steps, and he opened the door, letting her precede him into the house. Another minute and he'd be up the stairs to the isolation of his room. Sweat popped out on his forehead as a vision of her there with him flashed through his mind. He couldn't stop wanting her more than almost anything. But he also knew he couldn't cross that line. Hitting on someone who worked for him would make him as big an ass as his father, something he'd sworn never to be.

He set his keys in the basket on the table just inside the door, then met her gaze. "Good night, Grace."

But apparently fate wasn't going to let him off that easy. She didn't say a word, just smiled as she moved close. The scent of her skin was intoxicating and messed with his rational thoughts. This wasn't a good time to find out that it was true about the road to hell being paved with good intentions. When she stood on tiptoe and touched her mouth to his, he was a goner. He'd had better kisses, but there was something about the soft, sweet innocent pressure of Grace's kiss that pushed him over the edge.

Logan pulled her against him until their bodies were pressed together from chest to knee. Then he slid his fingers into her hair to make the pressure of their mouths firmer and proceeded to kiss the living daylights out of her. If he was going to hell anyway, why not make a detour to heaven first?

Chapter Eight

In some fuzzy part of her brain, Grace was aware that she'd never thrown herself at a man before, but she wasn't sorry. She'd thrown caution to the wind because she was tired of going along for the ride and wanted to drive this car. She wanted it more than she'd ever wanted anything ever, and life had a way of disappointing her. So now she kissed him back with all the longing she'd stored up. His mouth was everything she'd ever fantasized about and more—hot and demanding in the sexiest possible way. One breathless moan from her and his hold on her tightened—a good thing since her legs felt too wobbly to keep her upright.

He traced the seam of her lips with his tongue, and when she opened to him, he dipped inside. Every nerve ending in her body came alive and her skin grew hot and tingly. Then he kissed her cheek, chin and neck before taking her earlobe gently between his teeth. How was it possible to be so hot all over and not go up in flames?

His breathing was ragged as he skimmed the palms of his hands from her waist slowly up to her breasts, brushing his thumbs over each tip. She wanted desperately to feel him touch her bare skin, and a whimpery little sound came from deep in her throat.

Logan's eyes burned hot when his gaze touched her. His chest was heaving. "Grace?"

"W-what?"

"I'm going to take you upstairs to my bed. If that's not okay with you—"

She stood on tiptoe and kissed him on the mouth, mostly to stop the words, but partly because she was so thrilled that this was going exactly where she wanted it to. Especially because she hadn't thought he even liked her very much the way he'd been acting. "You talk too much. Has anyone ever told you that?"

One corner of his mouth quirked up. "No."

He took her hand in his and led her upstairs, flipping on the hall light before going into his room. Standing beside the bed, he put his hands on her shoulders and turned her. Then she felt his fingers at the back of her neck, undoing the dress's hook.

"What goes up must come down." His voice was rich and warm like chocolate, smooth and soft as velvet.

Grace could feel the material covering her back slowly separate, just before he pressed his mouth to the skin he'd just bared. She shivered in the most delicious possible way, then pulled her arms free of the dress before tugging the material over her hips to let it fall at her feet. She stepped out of it and kicked it aside before turning to face him.

"You probably could use some help with the man jewelry." She started removing the black-and-silver studs marching up the front of his crisp white dress shirt.

Wordlessly he held out one wrist then the other for assistance with the matching cuff links. After setting the hardware on the nightstand, she unbuttoned the shirt and he shrugged out of the wrinkled material, tossing it to the floor.

She settled her palms on his chest, letting the dusting of hair tickle her fingers. He was all lean, masculine muscle. Smiling up at him, she said, "All that ranch work has really paid off."

Grinning, he traced a finger from her collarbone to the top of one breast, just above her lacy bra. "And what do I have to thank for this?"

"Nothing." She laughed. "This is God given."

"And God is good."

He reached behind her and undid her bra with a twist of his fingers, and she let it fall to the floor between them. Next he took her bare breasts in his hands, and she thought, *Finally.* Her flesh seemed to swell from his touch, and when he brushed his thumbs over her again, a jolt of electricity flashed through her, headed straight to her girl parts. The knot of need in her belly tightened. Her eyes drifted closed, her chin tilted up and she moaned.

"Oh, God, Gracie. When you look like that I can't stand it. I can't wait—"

"Neither can I."

Logan threw back the spread and blanket on the bed and lowered her to the mattress. He shrugged off his socks and shoes, tuxedo trousers and briefs and moved into the bed beside her. She toed off her heels, and he settled his big palm on her midriff, then just looked at her.

"What?" She was so breathless she could barely speak.

"The first day you were here I surprised you while you were unpacking and you dropped all the panties you were holding." His tone was soft and seductive and scraped over her skin like a caress. "I've been thinking about those panties ever since. Seeing you in the pink ones—"

"I hope you're not disappointed," she whispered.

His eyes went dark and he shook his head, just a slight negative movement. "You're more beautiful than I imagined."

The words just melted her heart. She was nothing but putty in his hands, and she wanted him more than anything. She met his gaze, smiled, then lifted her hips and slid the small, silky scrap of pink material down her legs. "It's a real shame, then, that they have to come off."

He sucked in a breath and without a word rolled away and opened the nightstand drawer to retrieve something. Quickly, he ripped the square packet and put on the condom. The next moment she was in his arms and he was kissing her senseless with that wonderful mouth of his.

Gently he settled over her and nudged her legs apart before slowly entering her. Her breath caught and she savored the feel of him inside. Then he began to move, thrusting deeper, carrying her higher, stealing more breath. The intense pleasure started in her core and then rolled through her, picking up speed and power as it took over her mind, body, spirit. She clung to him, and he held her tenderly until the amazing storm passed.

And then he started to move within her again, pushing in more deeply, over and over. Suddenly he tensed, then buried his face in her neck as he groaned with satisfaction, finding his own release. She had no idea how long they stayed that way, but finally he lifted his head.

"I'm crushing you."

Before she could respond, he pushed himself up and rolled away, slipping out of bed. Moments later a light went on in his bathroom, then the door closed it off.

Grace must have dozed because when she opened her eyes, Logan was standing at the window, looking out. He'd put on sweatpants, and his whole posture looked just the opposite of relaxed, which was unexpected. Why hadn't he come back to bed? Not a post-sex cuddler?

That would have been too simple. She thought about just slipping away, pretending this never happened, but decided against that. It was like spotting a particularly nasty spider in the house and not dealing with it. You just kept thinking about when it was going to jump out and bite you.

She got up and grabbed his shirt, then slid her arms into it to cover herself. The only thing that would make this conversation worse was being naked for it. She crossed the distance between them and stopped beside him.

"So you're brooding. I can hear it. What are you thinking about, Logan?"

A long moment passed before he answered. "I wouldn't blame you if you quit."

"Why would I?"

"Because I'm your boss. I hit on an employee." He pressed his lips together for a moment. "That's the kind of thing my father would do. I'm no better than he is, and I swore I would not be a chip off the old block. Guess there's no fighting DNA."

"So, you're taking full responsibility for this?"

"Yes."

"Oh, brother." She shook her head. "First of all, I believe I, the employee, hit on you, the boss. For the record, you said good-night and *I* kissed *you*. In case you're wondering, I don't regret it in the least."

"Okay." But he didn't sound all that sure. "What else?"

"Hmm?"

"You said first. That implies there's more."

"Right. Second, I can't quit because I need this job."

"All the more reason I shouldn't have taken advantage of you."

"Don't go there." She folded her arms over her chest and looked out the window of his house. The moon bathed the outbuildings, land, lake and mountains in its silver light. This was all his, and she envied him. She wanted something of her own, too. "I made the decision to sleep with you, and I'm not an innocent, impressionable, vulnerable woman. I've been making my own decisions for a very long time now."

"Can't be that long. You're not that old."

Sometimes she felt ancient, and now was one of those times. "Right after I was born I was left at a fire station and never knew my parents."

He sucked in a breath. "Grace—"

"Don't interrupt me." She cut him off because the tone in that single word flirted with pity, and she wanted no part of that. "I went from one foster care situation to another. There were any number of reasons for the moves—personality clash, a job transfer, loss of job. Birth of their own child. It didn't matter to me because I knew early on the danger of expecting more. When change happened, I put my stuff in a plastic bag and went where they took me. At eighteen I aged out of the system and took care of myself." She could feel his gaze on her. "Why are you looking at me as if I have two heads?"

"I don't know. It's just—you're so cheerful all the time."

"That's a choice I make every day. Someone told me once that today isn't forever. That's true, and I made the decision to have a goal."

"Care to share?"

"Do you have any idea how lucky you are to have this land, this place to belong? The roots go deep." She glanced out the window again. "I want a house of my own with my name on the title. A place that no one can take away from me. That takes money."

"So that's why you can't quit."

"Yeah. This time it's going to happen."

"This time?" He frowned down at her.

"I was almost there before I got sidetracked by a man."

"What did he do?"

"Oh, it was my fault. He bought a fixer-upper house to flip and vaguely talked about love and someday marriage. I was so blinded by the glow of belonging that I gave him my savings, figuring we would do the project together, that it would bring us even closer."

"Obviously, something went wrong."

"When the house renovations were complete, he decided he didn't love me after all. We had no legally binding agreement, which meant I had no protection for my investment, no recourse for recovering my money."

"Geez, Grace—you got nothing?"

"Actually, that's not completely true. I got an expensive lesson. So, in case you were wondering, being stupid again over a man isn't part of my plan."

"Want me to beat him up for you?" There was enough menace in his voice to make one question whether or not he was kidding.

"No. I'm pretty sure that's against the law, and Cassie needs her dad not to be in jail."

"Even if her dad doesn't know that much about being a dad?"

"Let's be clear. You obviously have issues with your father, but from my perspective you're lucky to know who he is. What I said before about God-given assets—" She met his gaze. "I have no clue who gave them to me. You know where yours came from, the good, bad and ugly. And you have a connection to the land, something tangible that goes back generations. I envy you."

"When you put it like that…"

"Don't you dare pity me, Logan Hunt. I'm going to have property, too. When my job here is over, I'm going back to Buckskin Pass and buying a house."

"So, to sum up, you're saying that we should equally share the responsibility of having sex with no strings attached?"

That made her smile and she relaxed, just like one should

"FAST FIVE" READER SURVEY

Your participation entitles you to:
✳ 4 Thank-You Gifts Worth Over $20!

Complete the survey in minutes.

Get 2 FREE Books

See inside for details.

Dear Reader,

Since you are a lover of our books, your opinions are important to us... and so is your time.

That's why we made sure your **"FAST FIVE" READER SURVEY** can be completed in just a few minutes. Your answers to the five questions will help us remain at the forefront of women's fiction.

And, as a thank-you for participating, we'd like to send you **4 FREE THANK-YOU GIFTS!**

Enjoy your gifts with our appreciation,

Pam Powers

To get your
4 FREE THANK-YOU GIFTS:

✱ Quickly complete the "Fast Five" Reader Survey
and return the insert.

"FAST FIVE" READER SURVEY

1 Do you sometimes read a book a second or third time? ○ Yes ○ No

2 Do you often choose reading over other forms of entertainment such as television? ○ Yes ○ No

3 When you were a child, did someone regularly read aloud to you? ○ Yes ○ No

4 Do you sometimes take a book with you when you travel outside the home? ○ Yes ○ No

5 In addition to books, do you regularly read newspapers and magazines? ○ Yes ○ No

YES! I have completed the above Reader Survey. Please send me my 4 FREE GIFTS (gifts worth over $20 retail). I understand that I am under no obligation to buy anything, as explained on the back of this card.

235/335 HDL GMVN

FIRST NAME	LAST NAME

ADDRESS

APT.#	CITY

STATE/PROV.	ZIP/POSTAL CODE

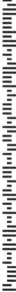

◀ If offer card is missing write to: Reader Service, P.O. Box 1867, Buffalo, NY 14240-8531 or visit www.ReaderService.com ▶

BUSINESS REPLY MAIL
FIRST-CLASS MAIL   PERMIT NO. 717   BUFFALO, NY

POSTAGE WILL BE PAID BY ADDRESSEE

READER SERVICE
PO BOX 1341
BUFFALO NY 14240-8571

NO POSTAGE
NECESSARY
IF MAILED
IN THE
UNITED STATES

after mind-blowing sex. "Only if *you* kiss *me*. Then we'll be even."

He did that and more.

The next morning Logan got out of the shower and looked in the steamy mirror. There was an actual grin on his face. He was choosing to take Grace at her word that she didn't hold him responsible for sex last night.

"Good thing," he said to his reflection. "Because I'd have to take the blame for two more times."

This shared blameworthiness worked for him.

The bed was empty when he woke up and now he smelled coffee, so his guess would be that she was downstairs. The grin on his face got wider, but that had to be about the prospect of coffee because one night with Grace didn't change anything. Well, maybe it changed a little since he didn't feel like putting his fist through the wall anymore.

He shaved, dressed and went downstairs. Grace was standing by the coffee maker and smiled when she saw him. Her eyes went all soft and glowy, and that made his chest feel tight. So that was another change.

"Wild guess," she said. "You're here for coffee."

"It's like you can read my mind."

"That makes me feel very powerful." She grabbed two mugs from the cupboard and filled both with the steaming, dark liquid. "Here you go."

He rounded the island and took the cup from her. "Thanks."

She looked so fresh and pretty. As far as he could tell, she wasn't wearing a lick of makeup. Her shiny, sun-streaked hair was pulled into a ponytail and her feet were bare. The white shorts and yellow T-shirt were the exact opposite of yesterday's wedding outfit with the sexy-as-sin pink pumps. Although he missed the zipper at half-mast, this was a good look, too. If he was being honest, he hadn't seen a look on her that didn't tie him in knots.

"So what do you want for breakfast? Pancakes, waffles, eggs, omelet?"

You? Logan didn't say the word out loud, but that didn't make it any less true. He wanted her again. He told himself that was no big deal. But he'd been with a lot of women and couldn't remember wanting even one of them so much, so soon.

"You pick," he said. "Don't go to a lot of trouble."

"How about bacon, eggs, toast, hash browns and juice?"

"Good. What can I do to help?"

She thought for a moment. "Set the table. Maybe toast and juice?"

"I can manage that," he said.

"Good to know you have skills."

The sexy, suggestive look she leveled at him had heat pooling low in his belly. And he was about to reach for her and show her his skills, but two things stopped him. His sister would be dropping Cassie off anytime, and he didn't want to start something he couldn't finish. It would be better if he and Grace had their clothes on when his daughter came home.

The other reason was about keeping last night a one-time thing. He was still her employer and didn't want to compromise her—even if she did take responsibility. But the way his gut tightened at the sight of her told him that resisting the attraction was easier said than done. Something he would worry about later.

"I can cook. In case you were wondering." He pulled plates and utensils from cupboards and drawers and put them on the table with place mats underneath.

"That's a relief. I don't have to worry about you starving to death out here all by yourself."

While Grace watched over the sizzling bacon and frying potatoes, Logan put bread in the toaster, ready to go when everything else was done. A feeling of fulfillment settled over him, maybe for the first time in his life. The only thing missing here was Cassie, and she'd be there soon.

Contentment apparently put him in a teasing mood. "Wow, you make me sound like an eccentric recluse with too many cats."

"Hmm. There was that recent litter." She broke eggs into a bowl and whipped them with a whisk. "I'd be careful if I were you."

"They're barn cats," he pointed out.

"Still—" She grinned, then tilted her head, listening. "Was that a knock on the door? I don't think I've heard anyone knock on the door before."

"It's probably Cassie." Funny, he'd just been thinking about her. Missing the little munchkin.

"Wouldn't she just come in? It's her house."

"Jamie's with her." And his sister might be showing caution because…why? Did she have some instinct about him and Grace? Some vibe of attraction that only a woman could see? Females were funny that way, picking up signals that men didn't notice. He hoped he was wrong and the door was simply locked.

Logan opened it, fully expecting Jamie's knowing grin, and would have preferred her merciless teasing to what was waiting for him.

"Hello, son." Foster Hart acted as if he dropped by every day and expected a warm welcome.

And he looked like he'd stepped out of a Viagra commercial. He was still handsome in a distinguished way with his silver-streaked dark hair, pressed jeans and navy blazer. He was trim and fit, and Logan hated the sight of him.

"What the hell are you doing here?"

"Nice to see you, too." His good humor never faltered. "It so happens that my niece and nephews, not to mention my children, have all relocated to Blackwater Lake. I'm here to see what all the fuss about this town is."

"The fuss is about family, and we both know that cramps your style. So, do us all a favor and go back to Dallas." Anger vibrated through him, leaving behind a hot, red haze.

"Look, Logan, however much you wish it wasn't so, I'm still your father. And I'd like to talk to you." The man walked right past him into the house, heading for the kitchen. "I have some things to say."

"Join the club," he muttered and shut the door.

He followed as fury and frustration balled in his belly. Then he remembered Grace. He was seconds behind Foster, who had stopped to give her the once-over. Logan went to stand beside Grace, wanting to push her safely behind him.

"So, who's this?" His father looked her over from head to toe, as if she was a prize mare at a horse auction. He glanced at Logan with a gleam in his eyes as if to say, *You're just like the old man.*

Logan's fingers curled into his palms as disgust trickled through him because that wasn't far off the mark. But before he could tell the man to go to hell, Grace spoke up.

"I'm Grace Flynn. I work for Logan, taking care of his daughter, Cassie, for the summer. While her mom is on her honeymoon."

"Yes, I heard Tracy was getting married. I'm sorry. Where are my manners?" He glanced at Logan before extending his hand to her. "I'm Foster Hart."

"Logan's father," she said. "It's nice to meet you."

"The pleasure is all mine." He looked smug that she knew who he was. "My reputation precedes me."

"It does," she said. "We were just about to have breakfast—"

"What do you want?" Logan interrupted because she was about to ask the bastard to join them. That wasn't going to happen.

"Where's Cassie?"

"She's not here," Logan snapped. And he wouldn't reveal that Jamie had her.

"When will she be back?" The man looked at Grace for an answer, as if sensing he'd get the information out of her.

"That's none of your business," Logan said.

"I'm only in town for the day. Business meeting in the morning," he shared with Grace. "I'd really like to see her."

"When hell freezes over." He couldn't stand the thought of this man anywhere near his child, damaging her the way he had his own kids. His protective instinct had been sharpened by experience and came from a painful place deep inside. There was no shutting it down now. "In case I haven't made it obvious, you're not welcome here."

The man's blue eyes narrowed. "She's my granddaughter."

"You really want to play the family card now? She's five and suddenly you show up?" Logan thought for a moment. "Oh, I get it. You found out her mom is away and figured to take advantage of the situation. Do an end run around her."

"It's a coincidence, but you've already made up your mind, so I won't waste my breath trying to change it."

"That might just be the only thing you've ever said that I agree with."

Foster looked at Grace. "Is he always so pigheaded?"

"He's a good father." She met his gaze.

Logan appreciated her vote of confidence and would take it even though the words were far from the truth. And he was done with this man.

"Please leave."

"She's my only grandchild. I have a right to see her."

"You gave up any rights you might have had when you treated my mother and your own children as if we were nothing. I won't let you do that to my child."

Foster stared him down for several moments as if weighing his options. Then he nodded, and there was something in his face Logan had never seen before. It looked like regret. Or remorse. Or both. But this was the man who had turned his back on family, so Logan figured lack of sleep had him seeing things that weren't there.

"It was a pleasure to meet you, Miss Flynn. Goodbye, son." The jovial facade was gone, replaced by an air of sadness, before he turned and left the room. Moments later the front door opened and closed.

Logan waited for a feeling of relief that his father was gone, but it didn't come.

"So…" Grace blew out a long breath and met his gaze. "That just happened."

"Yeah." He dragged his fingers through his hair. "The only good thing about it is that Cassie wasn't here."

"You know, Logan, he looked like he was sincerely disappointed about not seeing her."

"My father doesn't know the meaning of the word *sincere*. And we all need to learn to live with disappointment. I learned from him. The four of us learned that lesson really well." They grew up without a good father, and the scars of that affected all of them.

"People can change. Isn't it possible that he wants to make amends?"

"It's too late for that. He only thinks about himself. And I don't want that bastard to have anything to do with my daughter."

"It's been a lot of years." Her look was sympathetic. "You're not a kid anymore, and he's gotten older. Maybe he can see that he made mistakes. You're a good man—"

"Just stop, Grace. There's no question that he made mistakes. I'm a perfect example of his scorched-earth policy. Don't you get it? Did you see the way he looked at you? I'm that jackass's son. You just saw for yourself why it's a really bad idea to fall for me. Don't do it."

Logan had a bad feeling that warning was more for him than for her. He knew last night couldn't happen again, and his father dropping by was a reminder of why. Now he just had to figure out a way to forget how good sleeping with Grace had been.

The problem was, that would take a miracle. Even if he believed in them, he didn't deserve one.

Chapter Nine

Having a father—even a bad one—was better than no father at all. Take it from someone who never had one, Grace thought. It had been a couple of days since the ugly scene in Logan's kitchen, but she couldn't get it out of her mind. Probably because he had gone back to being distant and mostly absent.

Maybe that was for the best. The man she'd slept with and made breakfast for the next morning was a man who could get in the way of her goal to own a home and put down roots. That would not happen to her again.

"Grace?"

Cassie's voice pulled her back into the present. "What is it, sweetie?"

"Me and Paige and Emily are really thirsty."

Grace had set up a playdate because keeping Cassie happy was her primary responsibility. The three girls were playing on the grassy rise not far from the house. She was sitting on the porch steps supervising, ready to intervene diplomatically if necessary or just remain on emergency standby if not. Since the girls were interacting beautifully together, she had very little to do but contemplate the handsome rancher and his fondness for ignoring her after really hot sex.

"Does everyone like lemonade?" she asked them.

"Yes!" three little voices answered simultaneously and put an exclamation point on the response.

"And maybe some cheese and apple slices, too? You ladies need to keep your energy up." Grace stood to go inside.

The three girls looked at each other and nodded. Then Cassie spoke for the group. "Yes, please."

"Coming right up."

Grace walked into the kitchen to gather up food and drinks. There was a window overlooking the play area, and she glanced outside frequently to make sure the girls were okay. It was closing in on the time for Paige and Emily to be picked up, but she didn't know when the girls were scheduled to eat dinner. A healthy snack would get them through.

When she had everything together and three plastic glasses of lemonade poured, she set the items on a tray and carried it outside. The girls saw her and ran over to the porch, where Cassie's play table was set up for them.

"It's so hot." Dark-haired Paige was very dramatic.

Emily was a little redhead with the most adorable freckled face. "I'm so thirsty."

"This should help." Grace put a red plastic glass in front of her. Paige's was green, and Cassie got her favorite pink. "But if anyone is still thirsty when this is gone, I'll bring out some ice water."

"I wish we could have cookies." Cassie gave her the pitiful puppy-dog stare.

Grace held in a smile. At first this particular expression had made her want to ignore common sense and give this lovable child anything in the universe. Now she was emotionally invested and wanted what was best. Cookies this close to dinnertime wasn't it.

She squatted down between Paige and Cassie. "Moms will be here soon to pick up the girls and I don't think they would be happy if you spoiled your appetites."

"No," Emily agreed. "When I stay at my dad's on the weekend, he always takes me for ice cream before he brings me back to my mom. I can't eat my dinner, and Mommy gets so mad."

Sounded like the little girl's father was deliberately provoking his ex. But she stood by her theory that a dad in the picture was better than none at all. A grandfather, too. Grace happened to think Logan's dad regretted the past and wanted to do better with his granddaughter.

"Well, I think your mom will be okay with this snack," Grace assured her.

Emily nodded enthusiastically. "She likes me to have apples, and this cheese tastes really good."

"And so does the lemonade," Paige chimed in.

"Grace makes the best," Cassie said.

"Aw, you are too sweet, kiddo." She couldn't help it. She dropped a kiss on top of the little girl's head.

The sound of a car coming slowly up the drive made Grace look in that direction. It parked in the space near the porch, and Emily's mother exited the vehicle. The little girl definitely took after her redheaded mom. Wendy Anderson must have come from a yoga class, judging by her black, pink-trimmed spandex capri leggings and matching racerback top.

She waved and smiled, then joined them on the porch. And the very attractive woman was a walking exercise advertisement. She looked fabulous; there wasn't an ounce of fat on her or a hint of flab anywhere on that toned body.

She kissed her daughter, then met Grace's gaze. "Hi."

"Hi, Wendy."

The woman glanced at the blanket, dolls and other toys scattered on the grass. "They were busy. How was Emily?"

Grace smiled. "Perfect."

"No, really. I'm not one of those moms who believes her child can do no wrong."

"Your attitude is very refreshing. Take it from a kindergarten teacher," Grace said. "And, while I know she's probably not always perfect, she was today."

"Good. I've always said that if she's going to push the limits of perfection, I'd rather it be with me."

"Very sensible."

"I talked to Paige's mom. Her husband surprised her with dinner out, so I'm picking up both girls." Wendy was looking past her daughter, in the direction of the ranch buildings. Logan had just left the barn and was walking toward them.

"Do I hafta go right now, Mommy? I haven't finished my snack yet."

"That's up to Grace," Wendy said, looking at her.

"It's completely fine with me. There's no hurry."

"Okay." The other woman glanced at the rancher still walking this way. There was a hint of feminine interest in her eyes and a sassy swing in her toned hips when she headed in his direction. "I want to talk to Logan for a minute."

Grace experienced a stab of jealousy before she managed to tamp it down. He was a single father with a daughter. Wendy was a divorced woman with a daughter. They had something in common. Let the flirting begin. It was no skin off her nose. She just worked here for the summer.

Wendy intercepted him by her car. "Hi, Logan."

"How've you been?"

"Great. Tracy's wedding was beautiful, don't you think?"

"Yeah. She seemed really happy."

The woman leaned her flawless butt against the fender of her SUV and slid her big, Jackie-O sunglasses to the top of her head. "I'm very envious that she managed to find such a supernice guy right here in Blackwater Lake."

Grace couldn't tell from this angle, but it wouldn't surprise her if some eyelash fluttering was going on. But she could see Logan's shoulders tense and the expression in his eyes when he glanced over at her. This unexpected meeting was making him acutely uncomfortable.

She wasn't proud of herself, but Grace was kind of enjoying his suffering. Served him right for disappearing emotionally after they'd gotten close. All it took to send him running back into his cave was one face-to-face with his father. Obviously, he preferred to be a lone wolf, so he could just do that now. And she got a great deal of satisfaction in watching him deal with weddings-on-her-mind Wendy.

"This town is growing fast," he said to the woman.

"I'm still thirsty," Emily interrupted, holding up her empty red plastic cup.

"Okay." Grace's first responsibility was to these kids, but how she hated missing even a part of what was going on in flirtation central.

On the upside, refilling glasses meant that Logan's suffering would go on just a little bit longer. She was pretty sure Wendy wouldn't object to her daughter getting a refill.

Grace hurried inside and grabbed a pitcher from the cupboard, then put ice and water in it. She walked back to the porch, and all three girls held up their empty glasses.

"Here you go." She poured water for all of them, then stood back to pick up the thread of Logan's conversation.

"There's a new yoga studio near the resort at Black Mountain."

"I know. My cousin Cal's wife owns it," he said.

"That's right. Justine Walker married Cal Hart on Christmas Eve last year. Then she opened her fitness business. I just came from there."

Logan looked at Grace with a hint of help-me-out-here in his eyes. "My sister, Jamie, says it's a great place."

"I like it." Suddenly Wendy straightened away from the

car. "The hard work really pays off. This is my revenge body."

"I'm sorry, what?" No doubt about it. He was squirming big-time now.

"Revenge body. My husband left me for someone else." She shrugged as if her meaning should be obvious to him. "Since the divorce I lost twenty pounds and went to Black Mountain Bikram Yoga and Fitness. You're a man and I'd like your opinion. Do you think this will make my ex have second thoughts about dumping me?"

Logan looked at Grace for the third time, and there was panic mixed with pleading in his eyes. It would just be mean to ignore that, so pity topped payback and she decided to help put an end to his torment.

"Drink up, girls. We don't want to keep Mrs. Anderson any longer." Grace made sure her voice was loud enough to be heard. "Next time we have a playdate maybe we can go see the baby horse."

"I named him Prince Eric, like in *The Little Mermaid*." Cassie held up her pink glass. "I'm all finished."

"Me, too," Emily said. "Can we see the baby horse now?"

Grace met Logan's gaze, just to remind him who was in control. "I think he might be eating dinner. And a lot of activity might upset him. But we can have another playdate soon. Right, Wendy?"

"Definitely." She smiled at Logan. "Girls, time to go."

They all went down the porch steps to the car. Emily walked up to her mother and slapped a small five-year-old hand on that rock-hard thigh. "Me and Paige are ready to go."

If Wendy's parade was rained on, she didn't let it show. "Did you guys thank Grace for everything?"

"Thank you, Grace," the two said in singsong voices loud enough to be heard in Buckskin Pass.

"You're very welcome."

Wendy made sure both girls were secure in car seats, then smiled and waved. "Thanks, Grace. Nice to see you again, Logan."

Cassie stood between the two of them as they all watched the SUV turn and drive slowly back down the road.

"I like her." Grace found that was actually true. But she couldn't resist poking the bear. "Logan, don't you think Mrs. Anderson is nice?"

"Yes."

"Daddy?" Cassie looked up at him. "When can Emily and Paige come back to play?"

"That's up to Grace." He met her gaze. "Because that day I'll be really busy until very late doing some important ranch work."

So he wasn't all that anxious to see Wendy again anytime soon. Before his daughter could start her pitch to hard sell pinning down a specific date, Grace pointed to the toys still scattered on the grass. "Time to put things away, sweetie."

"Do I hafta? I'm so tired."

"I'll help you. Just let me talk to your dad for a minute." She met Logan's gaze.

"Ookay." With a dramatic and decidedly put-upon air, the little girl picked up two dolls by their floppy arms and took them into the house.

When Grace was sure Cassie couldn't hear, she said, "You so owe me for bailing you out."

"I wouldn't have needed it if you hadn't decided they needed more water."

"No one is dehydrating on my watch," she said, firmly defending her actions. "I could have suggested a bathroom break before they headed out, but I didn't."

A little bit of horror trickled into his expression as it

sank in that the suggestion would have produced a much longer exposure to Wendy. "Okay. I owe you. What's it going to cost me?"

Grace thought for several moments. What she wanted wasn't for herself. It was for Cassie. "The price for helping you out is one tea party."

He frowned. "You can't be serious."

"And yet I am. Completely serious."

"Look, Grace, you know I'm no good at that—"

"Practice makes perfect. It will get easier if you flex those muscles." And she suddenly got a mouthwatering memory of the very impressive ones underneath his shirt. Her chest tightened, threatening to cut off her air, but she ordered herself to focus. "One tea party," she insisted, "or I call Wendy and set up another playdate—"

"Okay. Where and when?"

"Four o'clock tomorrow. Wear your formal jeans and boots. It's royal day. I'll be the one in a tiara."

The next afternoon Grace was nervous as four o'clock got closer. She didn't know whether or not to tell Cassie her father had agreed to show up for a tea party. That agreement did fall somewhere on the blackmail scale, but the end justified the means, right? Only if he followed through. If he didn't, his daughter would really be disappointed, but only if she knew it was a possibility in the first place.

Right now Grace was sitting with Cassie on the top front porch step and the little girl had her face resting in her hands, the personification of boredom.

"You've got some coloring books and brand-new crayons," Grace pointed out.

"I don't want to color."

"We could play hide-and-seek," Grace suggested.

"No." Cassie's voice completely lacked enthusiasm. "It's no fun with just two people. And you always let me win."

"I guess I do." She thought for a moment. "We could go swimming in the pool or take a walk down by the lake and skip stones on the water."

"I'm too tired."

The screen door behind them opened and a familiar deep voice said, "Then I guess you're too tired for a tea party."

Logan walked over to them and took a seat on the other side of his daughter. The clean, fresh male scent of him drifted to Grace and burrowed inside her, making her feel all tingly and warm. Every nerve ending was fired up and dancing like there was no tomorrow. His jeans weren't formal and the boots were scuffed, but his hair was still damp from a shower. He'd cleaned up for the occasion, and Grace hadn't been sure he would show up at all. Until he did.

"What are you doing here, Daddy?"

"I was told there would be a tea party at four sharp." Over his daughter's head he met Grace's gaze. "Where's your tiara?"

"Darn," she said. "It's at the cleaners."

"Wouldn't you know. On royal day, too." His eyes were teasing.

"Don't you have work to do?" Cassie was still skeptical.

"There's always something to do on a ranch," he said, "but it can wait until tomorrow."

Cassie glanced from Logan to Grace, and excitement was catching fire in eyes that were the same color as her father's. "You're really gonna play tea party with me?"

"Yes. Is it okay if Grace stays, too?"

"Yes!" She stood and threw her arms around him, as far as they would go. Which wasn't far considering how broad his shoulders were.

Grace's throat closed with emotion because the picture

they made was just about the sweetest thing ever. Only someone with a heart two sizes too small wouldn't be moved by it.

But Cassie was too excited about this unexpected development to let the quiet moment last very long. "Do you want the tea party inside or outside?" she asked her father.

"Where do you want it?"

"Outside."

"Then let's do it right here. I guess we need your table and chairs."

"Yes. Can you get it, Daddy? You're stronger than Grace."

"I think I can manage that."

"I'm going to bring out the dishes." Cassie raced into the house.

Before Logan followed her, he said to Grace, "She gives orders like a general."

"You noticed. If you know what's good for you, you'll get right on moving that table," she told him.

"Family pack animal," he muttered, easily rolling to his feet.

With everyone pitching in, it wasn't long until everything was set up. Cassie took a seat and Grace folded herself into one of the small chairs. Uncertainly, Logan looked down at the one in front of him.

"How come you're not sitting, Daddy?"

"I'm afraid I'll break it."

"You are kinda big," she allowed.

"I know what we can do." Grace wouldn't let something like an undersized chair ruin the moment. "He can sit on the step stool you use in the kitchen to reach the sink."

The little girl's face lit up like a fireworks finale on the Fourth of July. She jumped to her feet and headed for the front door. "That's a great idea. I'll get it."

"I should have gone," he said. "It might be too heavy for her."

"She's the hostess and takes it very seriously. If she needs help, she'll ask."

"If you say so." But he didn't look sure.

When Cassie appeared with the stool that was almost as big as she was, Logan opened the screen door and said, "Can I help you with that?"

"Thank you," she said politely, letting him take it from her. "Put it right there, across from Grace."

He followed orders, then sat. Even with the alternative chair, the child's table in no way accommodated his tall form. His daughter could not have cared less. She was clearly happy as could be.

"Do you like tea, Prince Adam?" she asked, in full pretend mode, as she picked up the pink toy teapot and looked at her father.

Grace could see he had no clue what was going on and decided to help him out. "Prince Adam is also known as the beast from *Beauty and the Beast*. At first he's selfish and impatient because he was so spoiled. But after living as the beast, he becomes kind and brave. Cass and I were reading about him just last night."

"The beast?" His look was wry. "Typecasting?"

"What does that mean?" Cassie's confusion made her look so much like Logan.

"It means," Grace said, "giving someone a part to play that is a lot like their real-life personality."

"Daddy's kind and brave, so he can be Prince Adam." She looked at him. "Do you like tea?"

He hesitated for a moment. "I'm more of a coffee guy, but whatever—"

"Prince Adam likes tea," Cassie said confidently as she poured the pretend liquid into the cup in front of him.

Logan looked clumsy and ill at ease. It was a good bet that he was wishing to be anywhere but here.

"I'd like tea, Princess Cassandra." Grace was trying to distract attention from his awkwardness. "It's a beautiful day for a tea party. And don't you think Lady Barbie looks thirsty? I know she likes her tea with milk and sugar."

"I think you're right, Princess Jasmine," Cassie agreed. Then she poured pretend tea all around.

And the little girl was off and running. She chattered away, offering milk and sugar to everyone. She talked about the upcoming ball at the palace and hoped she didn't lose her glass slipper and that her coach didn't turn back into a pumpkin. She was going to live happily-ever-after with the prince.

Grace interjected things here and there, to move the make-believe narrative along, and she was pretty sure Cassie never noticed that her father perfectly played the strong, silent type. And he continued to look stiff and uncomfortable. Her heart went out to him. He was deeply and sincerely concerned about messing Cassie up and put so much pressure on himself to be perfect, to always do the right thing. But in a situation like this there was no wrong.

"Lady Barbie is tired. I'm going to find Princess Aurora to take her place." Cassie made the announcement, then went inside the house.

Logan blew out a sigh of relief as he looked at Grace. "I can't do this."

"Define *this*."

"Play with her," he said. "I feel like a bull rider in a crystal shop. I'm a fraud, and she knows it."

"Logan, you have to relax. This is not something that will send her into therapy. She won't remember what you did or didn't say. Just get in touch with your inner child."

"That's just it. I don't think I ever was a child. I was the oldest. I took care of the younger ones." He dragged his fingers through his hair. "That didn't leave a lot of time to just be a kid."

She might have cut him some slack if her own upbringing hadn't been difficult, too. "It's never too late to learn how to be a kid. The fact is that you're just a prop. A placeholder. Cassie is doing all the imagining."

"I should do something. I feel useless," he said.

"You're so wrong about that. Being here *is* doing something. You're bonding with your daughter. You don't even have to say anything." She thought for a moment and came up with a few pointers. "Maybe an occasional 'Oh?' just to show interest. Or ask how many horses Prince Adam has. She'll take that and run with it."

"I don't know." He rested his elbows on his knees. "It doesn't seem like enough."

"It is, Logan. I promise. All you ever have to do is show up. It's impossible to go wrong doing that."

Cassie returned with another doll and propped her in the empty chair. "I couldn't find Princess Aurora. This is Princess Jane. She was in time-out, but she said she was sorry for not picking up her toys. So I let her come to the tea party."

Comprehension dawned in Logan's eyes. He was getting that his little girl was incorporating her real-life experiences into this make-believe world. He met Grace's gaze, then took a deep breath.

"I bet Princess Jane is happy to be here."

"She is, Daddy—I mean Prince Adam. And she promised she'll always pick up after herself from now on." Cassie poured pretend tea for the newcomer.

"May I have some more tea?" he asked.

"Yes, you may." The little girl smiled at him.

He picked up his cup and acted as if drinking from it. "This is very good. But it's a little hot."

"Be careful," Cassie warned. "Don't burn yourself. Just blow on it first."

Grace watched him make an effort. It wasn't elegant, natural or effortless, but he was trying. He was *there*. She realized that's the kind of man he was. If he gave his word, he would keep it—even if he looked silly with his big hand dwarfing a tiny pink teacup as he sipped imaginary tea.

Grace felt her heart squeeze tight. If only that was her imagination, but she knew it was all too real. Her feelings were tipping into dangerous territory, and she wasn't quite sure how to make them stop.

Chapter Ten

"And the handsome prince and beautiful princess lived happily-ever-after." Grace closed the bedtime book she'd read to Cassie then leaned over to give her a hug and kiss on the forehead. "And now it's time to go to sleep, Princess Cassandra."

Logan never got tired of watching this nighttime ritual. He was glad his daughter had a bed, a roof over her head and enough to eat. She was safe. Unlike him before his family had come to the ranch. There was no having friends over to the house because there wasn't one. He'd slept with one eye open in a car on the street, thanks to dear old dad.

"I need a good-night kiss, Daddy."

"I thought you'd never ask." He straightened away from the doorway and traded places with Grace. "Isn't it lucky that I have a good-night kiss to spare?"

She held out her little arms to him, and he sat on the edge of the bed to lean over and hug her. "I love you, baby girl."

"I love you, too, Daddy. It was so much fun playing tea party with you today."

He'd felt like a fish out of water. Nothing about his childhood had prepared him to play make-believe. He'd been too busy living in the real world, where survival meant knowing what was really going on around you.

"I'm sure Paige and Emily are better at playing than me."

"No." Cassie shook her head. "Because they're not boys. There's no one to play the prince."

"Glad to help."

"You are a really good Prince Adam," she told him.

At five, her standards weren't very high, but he liked being her hero. Still, that would last only until the next time he screwed up. It was inevitable, no matter what Grace had said about showing up being enough.

"Can you play with me again tomorrow?"

"I can't, honey." Who knew the screwup opportunity would present itself so soon? She was too little to understand that there were things that needed to get done on a ranch as big as his. "I had to put off some chores so that I could play today. That means I have to work a little longer tomorrow. I have to take care of the horses."

"I know you're busy, Daddy. But since you have to do stuff with the horses tomorrow, maybe you could teach me to ride."

Logan heard a sound from Grace, who was still standing in the doorway, and knew she was trying not to laugh. It was obvious even to him that he'd walked right into that one.

"It's getting late, Cassie." Grace's voice was firm but gentle. "Time to turn out the light."

"But what about riding?" the little girl protested.

Logan sighed. "We'll talk about it."

"That's what you always say," she grumbled. "But we never do."

He leaned forward and kissed her forehead. "Sleep tight, you."

"Night, Daddy. Night, Grace."

"Good night, sweetie. See you in the morning."

Logan turned off the bedside lamp. "Sweet dreams, Princess."

He backed out of the room and pulled the door halfway closed, then followed Grace downstairs. Watching the feminine sway of her hips made him wonder if that might just be the finest-looking rear view he'd ever seen. Nice butt. And those snug, worn jeans hugged her hips and legs, outlining them to perfection.

It had been a week since the wedding, and therefore a week since making love to her. He'd thought staying away as much as possible would make him want her less, but he'd been wrong. It seemed to get worse whether he saw her or not. Maybe the not-having-her wouldn't be so bad if he hadn't slipped up that one time. Her taking responsibility didn't really alleviate his guilt. She was still his employee and he should have stopped. That was his bad.

In the kitchen Grace filled a cup with water, then put it in the microwave. She glanced over her shoulder and smiled. "I'm having real tea. Want some?"

That made him smile. "I'm more of a coffee guy."

"I can make a fresh pot for you."

"It was a stressful day. I need something stronger."

She leaned back against the cupboard while waiting for the water to heat. "The pressure of playing Prince Adam?"

"Yes."

But mostly he felt the strain of having to resist her. What combination of characteristics drew him to her like a moth to flame? Her hair? Pretty, but there were a lot of pretty brunettes out there. Her eyes? Hazel with flecks of gold and brown, colors that changed when she was happy, disappointed or just being thoughtful. Her smile? God knew he would do almost anything to get one out of her. The trim body? He highly approved. The package was attractive, but when you threw in that quirky personality…

The microwave went off and she pulled out the steaming mug, then dropped in a tea bag. She noticed him watching her, and the pulse in her neck jumped.

"You're sure you don't want some tea? It's supposed to help you sleep."

"I'll pass."

Logan grabbed a tumbler from the cupboard and a bottle of Scotch from above the refrigerator. After pouring a small amount into his glass, he took a sip. The liquid scalded all the way to his belly but did nothing to put out the fire burning there.

They were facing each other, not even standing all that close, but he swore he could feel the heat of her body, smell the scent of her skin.

"So…" She blew on the steam rising from her mug. "You did good today."

"If you mean looking like a complete dope, then I agree with you." He took another sip of Scotch.

"Yeah. Just so you know, the video will be on YouTube." She grinned. "You might have *felt* like a dope, but to your daughter you hung the moon."

"She's five."

"True. And she would have been ecstatic if you had sat there like a vegetable, or grunted like a caveman."

That made him smile. "Prince Adam has standards after all. He would never stoop that low."

"And that just highlights my point. Even playing make-believe you have principles."

"Not being a Neanderthal isn't all that high a bar," he said wryly.

"Cassie's bar is just you being there. So, I say again, you did good, Logan." She sipped her tea, and a twinkle in her eyes turned them gold. "Did you notice how she pushed her advantage about learning to ride when you mentioned the horses?"

"Give her an inch and she'll take a mile." *A chip off the old block*, he thought. Grace gave him a kiss and he took her to bed. His gut knotted at the memory, part guilt, part hunger.

"You really should teach her," Grace said. "Her mom lives in town, but this ranch is part of her world. Her heritage. How wonderful that she has it."

"I'm not sure she's the right age—"

"When did you learn to ride?"

"Twelve. Granddad taught me when we came to live here on the ranch."

Grace was studying him. "Your face just lit up. Why? Was it learning to ride, or just being with your grandfather?"

"Both. He was tough as leather but a good man. He loved my mom and would do anything for her. And actually did when he took all of us in." He tossed back the last of his Scotch, then stared into the bottom of the empty glass. "He said I took to riding a horse pretty well but it would have been easier and I'd have picked it up faster if I'd started when I was younger."

"Like five?"

He met her gaze. "That's just mean, piling on like that. Taking Cassie's side."

"You threw me a bone and I went with it." She didn't look sorry at all. "It's something to think about."

"It was a low blow using my words against me. And yet, wise. How did you get so smart, Grace Flynn?"

"A very good question." She set her cup on the counter beside her and folded her arms over her chest. "I went from foster home to foster home and then a group placement. Unlike you, I didn't have any family who taught me things."

Logan realized that from time to time he felt sorry for himself because of the bad stuff that happened in his childhood. But when he thought about how much worse Grace had it growing up, he realized he had no right to self-pity.

She sure didn't go there. "The people who took you in must have been good."

"Yeah. And I could say the same for you." She gave him a pointed look. "Your mother and grandfather showed you right from wrong and how to apply those lessons to your own life."

Logan set his glass on the island and toyed with it. "But there's no escaping your DNA."

Her eyes turned dark, more brown than green, a shade of hazel hidden until now. "At least you can put names and faces to your DNA. I can't do that because no one wanted me."

He saw the sadness and anger that she usually hid beneath a perky smile. Life had knocked her around, but she still managed to be sweet, smart and funny. And so desirable.

"I want you."

Her eyes widened. "What?"

As soon as the words came out of his mouth, Logan wanted them back. "Grace, I didn't—I shouldn't have—"

"It's all right. I can see the *but* in your eyes. And I get it. You're fighting your DNA."

"Giving in to it would make me just like him."

"The man you detest," she said.

He nodded. "By extension I would hate myself. And I don't want to compromise you any more than I already have."

For a split second her eyes said, "What if I want to be compromised?" Then she sighed and nodded. "I understand, Logan."

"Okay. Good. I'm glad."

"I'll take my tea upstairs." She picked up her cup and headed out of the room, then stopped. "You told Cassie you had to work late with the horses, but it's my afternoon off. Will that mess you up?"

"No. Thanks for the reminder. I'll rearrange my chore schedule. Cassie and I can go see a movie."

"Okay, then. Good night." She walked away without looking at him.

Logan stood there for a long time feeling like crap. Why did doing the right thing feel so damn wrong? The fact that Grace was so understanding about why he couldn't touch her again should have been a relief.

It wasn't. And the loneliness pouring through him was proof.

Grace realized an afternoon off wasn't all it was cracked up to be. She'd gotten used to doing things with Cassie, and now being on her own felt...lonely. There was something special about the little girl and she loved being with her. She'd have happily given up this time by herself, except that it was important for Cassie to be with her father.

Today Grace had explored a little more of Blackwater Lake and liked the community even more. In a refurbished barn painted red with white trim, there was a thrift/antiques store on the side of the road as you drove into town. The items inside were all donations and the profit went into The Sunshine Fund, which helped people going through a rough patch financially to get back on their feet.

Now she was browsing the shops on Main Street. April Kennedy's photography store showcased pictures the owner had taken of local scenery—the lake, mountains and meadows of wildflowers. She'd chatted with April, whose biggest problem was who would be taking the wedding photos when she married Sheriff Will Fletcher in a couple of months. Quality problem from Grace's perspective.

She'd spent a lot of time trying to decide whether she

liked the black-and-white or color prints better. And all that thinking had made her hungry. Now it was too late for lunch and too early for dinner, so she decided the perfect compromise was ice cream. One perk of being an adult was that you could make your own decision about spoiling your appetite. Not that anyone had cared all that much about her appetite when she was a kid.

Potter's Ice Cream Parlor was close and she walked to it, feeling virtuous about burning off calories before indulging. Her thighs weren't rock hard, but no one was perfect. She walked into the cheerful little shop adjacent to the Harvest Café. Just in front of her was the cold case with a glass front where the ice cream was displayed.

Little circular tables and chairs with the backs shaped like hearts filled the center of the store for customers to sit and eat. Prints of various sundaes and multicolored sprinkles were on the walls. The place was empty except for a young mother with two children, one in an infant carrier. And she looked familiar.

She was Logan's cousin. Grace had met her on the Fourth of July here in town. "Ellie?"

The woman turned. It took a beat or two, but Ellie McKnight finally smiled when recognition dawned. "Grace. Hi. Sorry. Took me a second to put your face and name together. I used to be quicker than that. I think it's called mom-brain."

"Probably has more to do with sleep deprivation. Your baby boy is beautiful." She smiled at the sleeping infant in the carrier.

"Thank you."

"Honestly, I'm surprised you even remember me. You get extra points for that because it was so brief and pretty chaotic during the Independence Day celebration."

"In a town like Blackwater Lake it's the new faces that

stand out. Plus you work for my cousin. Of course I re-member you."

"That's very nice of you to say even if it's not true," Grace said.

The teenage girl working behind the counter came out of a back room. Her name tag said Tiffani.

"Sorry. I didn't know anyone was here. What can I get you?"

"Can I have vanilla, Mommy?" her little girl asked.

"Of course, sweetie."

Ellie gave her order, then looked sheepishly at Grace. Her voice was too low for the child to hear. "I know I'm a horrible mom. Ice cream so close to dinner is bad. But I'm starving and I know Leah is, too. I think breaking a rule every once in a while is not an official Mom fail. In fact, maybe it's okay not to be rigid all the time."

"I agree."

But Logan wouldn't. Relaxing control meant he was turning into his father. It was black or white. No gray area. No wiggle room.

Tiffani set a small cup with a scoop of vanilla on the counter. "Here's one."

"Thanks." Ellie took it and walked over to a table with the kids. She set the infant seat on the floor, then lifted Leah to a chair and put the ice cream in front of her. "Be right back, love."

"Okay, Mommy." The little girl took the plastic spoon and started to eat.

When Ellie returned to the glass case, another cup of ice cream was ready for her. She paid the bill and picked up her treat. "Where's Cassie?"

"It's my afternoon off," Grace said. "That means father/daughter movie day because heaven forbid he try some-thing new with her."

"Is there a problem?" Ellie looked sympathetic.

"Did I say that last part out loud?" Accidentally on purpose. Classic passive-aggressive. Grace sighed. "No. Everything is fine. Well, it's not really fine, but it's none of my business."

"That sounds like something that needs some discussion," the other woman commented. She looked at the cup in her hands. "But there isn't anything ice cream and girl talk can't fix. Come on over and sit with us when you get yours."

Ellie walked away before Grace could politely decline the invitation, and by the time she'd paid for her salted caramel and vanilla sundae, talking seemed like an excellent idea. Plus she really liked this woman.

Grace sat down across from her. Leah was between them, completely absorbed in alternately eating her ice cream and playing with it.

"So," Ellie said, "how are you liking it here in Blackwater Lake?"

Grace knew that was a general lead-in to talk about Logan, but she decided to go with it. "I'm very impressed. I saw the thrift store today and love the idea of funneling that money into a fund that helps people."

"Yeah. It's a really special project. My brother Sam owns Hart Financial and is in charge of administering the fund."

"Don't you have two other brothers?"

"Yes. Lincoln is in real estate development with my husband, Alex. Cal owns Hart Energy. They both recently relocated here from Dallas." Ellie's voice was filled with pride as she mentioned her family.

"You're very lucky to have siblings." Grace couldn't stop the spurt of envy, so she might as well cop to it. "I'm an only child."

"I am very grateful for my brothers," she admitted.

"That's not always how I felt when we were growing up, however. But the three of them have had my back more than once. And I hope I've done the same for them."

"That's nice."

"And speaking of family," Ellie said. "How are you liking working for my cousin Logan?"

"Cassie is a sweetie. She makes the job easy. In fact, it doesn't feel like work."

"So, your reservations regarding the situation are all about Logan?"

Grace was kind of hoping they were going to skip over her little outburst. "Oh, I'm really not entitled to an opinion."

"And yet you have one." Ellie smiled. "What was it you said? Something about him not trying something new. There was a tone in your voice, and I'd bet you have a lot to say on the subject."

"That's the thing. I've already talked to him about shaking things up, making Cassie part of what he does on the ranch. But he's one stubborn cowboy."

"It's in the genes." Ellie noticed something in Grace's expression. "What did I say?"

"Do you know Logan well?"

"We're first cousins, but our fathers couldn't be more different. Logan's mother left with her children because Uncle Foster is a serial cheater. We didn't see them for years after that. But now we're all here in Blackwater Lake. We've reached out, met him at Bar None, the local pub, trying to reconnect."

"He actually showed up?"

"It was kind of a surprise to us, too," Ellie admitted. "I was hopeful that his presence meant he had an open mind about being part of the family again. Apparently he was just there in body but not in spirit because he's back to keeping to himself."

"Really?"

Ellie nodded. "We make sure to invite him to all the family holiday gatherings, but he never shows. And his siblings kind of follow his example."

"I guess the wounds their father inflicted are too deep. Being homeless had to have been tough."

"So you know about that?"

"Yes." Grace sighed. "And I met Foster Hart."

Ellie's eyes widened. "When?"

"The day after Tracy's wedding. He showed up unexpectedly at the ranch to see Cassie."

"How did that go?"

Grace would never forget the fury in Logan's eyes or the warning in his voice. "Not a Kumbaya moment."

"I can't really blame Logan. Uncle Foster brought it all on himself. Actions and consequences."

"I get that. But the funny thing is," Grace said, "it looked to me as if he's genuinely sorry about alienating his son. And he seems to really want to see his granddaughter. Get to know her."

"What did Logan say?"

"Putting it mildly, he said that Foster shouldn't hold his breath about that ever happening."

Ellie nodded thoughtfully. "So it's not just my brothers and me Logan is rejecting."

"Apparently not."

"I get why he's angry at his dad. What they went through before settling with their grandfather here in Blackwater Lake was pretty terrible. But the rest of the family didn't hurt him. We're trying to embrace him."

"Like I said. The wounds go pretty deep."

"So he's refusing to have anything to do with anyone

named Hart except his brothers and sister," Ellie mused. "I know he goes by his mother's maiden name of Hunt, but I was hoping time was smoothing the rough edges of his resentment. It would seem that's not the case."

"On the upside, he's trying not to be like his father. Everything he does is about protecting Cassie."

"That's all well and good," Ellie said. "But as she gets older, she's going to want answers about why she has relatives close by but never sees them. It's not necessary to protect her from us. We would never hurt her."

"I'm sure he knows that on some level. And really, the whole movie thing is about limiting his interaction with Cassie so *he* doesn't hurt her somehow. He doesn't trust his DNA. And it's not just about his daughter. He's insulating himself from anything that could touch him emotionally."

"Including you?"

"What?" Grace met the other woman's gaze.

"If you were talking to one of my brothers they would miss it because they're men after all. But you can't hide it from another woman." Ellie's voice was gentle. "You have feelings for Logan."

"Not on purpose."

"It never is." Ellie's tone was sympathetic. "And?"

"He's so worried about becoming his father that he completely rejects feeling at all. Except for Cassie."

"Oh, Grace—"

She half listened to the other woman's supportive words, but her mind was spinning with what she'd just heard. Things with Logan were worse than she'd thought. She knew he was keeping her at arm's length, but she was the hired help. He wouldn't hit on her and risk being like his father.

But Logan was turning his back on family, too. Grace would give almost anything to have brothers, sisters, cousins, aunts and uncles. He had that and was pushing them away, refusing to give his cousins a chance, and her heart just ached for him. Not just him—Cassie, too. She deserved a chance to know them.

He was hurting himself even more, and she just couldn't stand that. Grace was going to do something. And it would start with father/daughter bonding that didn't involve sitting in a dark movie theater where talking was frowned on.

Chapter Eleven

Logan got up for work every morning at about the same time as God, but it would be a miracle if God made coffee. So why did he smell it on the way downstairs?

He walked into the kitchen, and the mystery was solved. "Grace. What are you doing up?"

"We need to talk."

Those four words struck fear into the soul of every man who heard them. Logan was no exception. "Can it wait until later? I really have to—"

"No. It can't wait. And you're probably going to want coffee first. Can I fix you some eggs or pancakes?"

That was a hard decision. He really liked her cooking, but if the price for eating was hearing something he wouldn't like, it might not be worth a pancake party in his mouth.

"I'll just have coffee," he said.

"Okay." She wrapped her hands around the steaming mug on the table in front of her.

Logan couldn't help noticing that she was still dressed for bed with a short, satiny robe over her pajamas. His fingers tingled and palms itched to touch her bare skin. The devil of it was, he could have her. He knew it based on the way he caught her looking at him sometimes. But one of them had to be strong, and it looked like that chore fell to him. Because he didn't want to have Grace on his conscience.

He poured coffee and joined her at the table. Might as well get this over with. "What's on your mind? Must be important for you to get up this early to ambush me."

She ignored the ambush crack. "It's about Cassie."

Fear sliced through him for a second. "Is she all right?"

"She's fine. I didn't want her to overhear this conversation."

"Why?"

"Because it might upset her."

"But you don't mind upsetting me." He blew on the top of his steaming mug, then took a sip. "Am I supposed to know what you're getting at?"

"I guess I'm stalling. You're not going to like it. But I feel very strongly about this, Logan, and I absolutely can't let it slide—"

"Grace—your point?"

"Okay." She took a deep breath and met his gaze. "I think you should teach Cassie how to ride a horse."

"You're right."

"I am?" She blinked at him in surprise.

"I don't like it. And my answer is still the same. Not until she's older."

Grace's chin lifted, a tell that her stubbornness was kicking in. "I don't care whether or not you like it or what your answer still is. Cassie wants to ride, and no one is more qualified than you to teach her."

Logan studied her. Last night when he and Cass got back from the movie, he'd sensed something different in Grace. She'd looked either sad or angry or both and then seemed to make up her mind about something that she was wrestling with. Apparently that something was this.

"I think that decision is one that should wait until her mom is home," he argued.

"I disagree. You're her father and have every right to choose a healthy activity while Cassie is in your care."

"And I'm choosing the healthiest alternative, which is not to teach her." Logan could see why Grace didn't want his daughter around for this talk, and he appreciated her sensitivity. This would be so much worse if he was fighting Cassie, too.

"Logan, it would be good for so many reasons. One of the most important would be to bring the two of you closer."

He had a stubborn streak of his own going on and dug into it. "We're just fine."

"Are you really?" The look in her eyes said she didn't think so. "That's a debate for another time. What's relevant to this conversation is that I'm willing to go to the mat on this."

"What does that mean?" he asked warily.

"I think teaching your daughter about riding a horse is so important that you'll have to fire me to get me to drop it."

He hadn't expected that, and from somewhere deep inside him he felt a resounding *no*. He didn't want her to go. "Why is this so important to you?"

"Because I know what it's like not to have a father."

"Cassie has me," he argued.

"Does she really, though?"

He didn't want to think too much about that and how close to right she was. There had to be a way to change her mind about this crazy idea. "If you go, what happens to the down payment for your house?"

"I've waited this long. I can wait a bit longer. But Cassie will only be little for a short time." Then a gleam stole into her eyes. "If I quit, you'd be forced to bring your daughter to work with you. Or not work at all, and we both know that can't happen. So, I'd like to be a fly on the wall and see you handle that."

"You don't think I can replace you?"

"Maybe. But in the meantime your carefully controlled life would be disrupted and you would be forced to spend time with her that isn't structured. That wouldn't be such a bad thing."

Yes, it would, he thought. Control equaled safety, and Grace had just held a match to the fuse of his carefully ordered life. Neither choice was good, and he wouldn't risk a bluff. After thinking it over, he figured ten minutes of a riding lesson was the least-bad option. Letting Grace go wasn't happening, and he flatly refused to even think about why he felt so strongly about that.

"Okay," he finally said. "You win."

"No. Cassie does. She's going to be so excited when I tell her. What time should I bring her down to the corral?"

"So we're doing this today?"

"You didn't really think I was going to put it off, did you?" She gave him a wry look.

"A guy can hope." He thought about his work schedule for the day. "Late afternoon would be best. And the horses are less frisky than early in the morning."

"Okay. Thank you, Logan."

The approval in her smile was almost worth the anxiety he felt about going against his instincts on this. He really hoped he didn't regret giving in to her extortion.

So, he went about his workday hoping the early morning scene in his kitchen had been a dream. At about four o'clock Logan had proof it wasn't. He saw Grace first. She was trying to keep up with his daughter, who was running toward him. Even from here he could see the look of pure joy on her face and wanted to keep it there forever.

"Daddy!" She came to a screeching halt on the other side of the fence from him and started climbing. When she got to the top, he lifted her down inside the corral. "Is that my horse?"

He glanced at the saddled pony standing patiently beside him. The animal was small and not so young anymore. He was well trained and mellow.

"Yes. This guy is Chocolate."

"Like candy. I like it," she said.

"Me, too." Grace arrived a second or two later. She stood on the bottom slat of the fence, looking at the dark brown horse. "Looks like a very serene fellow."

"He is." Logan met her gaze from beneath the brim of his Stetson. "You should come and meet him up close and personal."

"If you want moral support, all you have to do is ask." She climbed the fence and swung a shapely leg over the top, preparing to descend into the enclosure.

Logan couldn't resist the chance to touch her. He put his hands at her waist to lift her down.

"Thanks," she said.

"Daddy, I'm petting Chocolate. Is this the right way?"

For a split second he'd forgotten she was there. This was off to a bad start. "That's good, Cass. Let him get used to you."

"I want to sit on him." She looked up as if Logan had all the answers. "How do I get up there?"

This was the part he dreaded. No matter how small and calm the horse he'd chosen, his daughter was smaller and just the opposite of calm. On the animal's back was a long way down for her.

"When you get big enough, you put your foot in the stirrup, hold on to the saddle horn and pull yourself up."

"When will I be big enough?"

"Ten, maybe."

"But I want to ride today." She stuck her lip out in the beginning of a pout.

"I bet your dad is planning to lift you up." Grace gave him a look that said "nice try, but you're not getting out of this."

"So, you really want to sit on him?" Logan asked.

"Yes!"

"Okay." He swung her into his arms and settled her in the saddle before handing her the reins. "First-time riders usually hold them too high. Just rest your hands on the saddle horn. If you lift them, Chocolate will think you're giving him a command. Or the movement can pull on the bit in his mouth and hurt him."

"I would never hurt him, Daddy," Cassie said sincerely.

"I know you wouldn't," he assured her. "Now sit up straight. Don't slouch."

"Does she need to grip with her knees and thighs?" Grace asked a little anxiously.

"You've been watching too many Westerns." He glanced over his shoulder. "Clenching is tiring for the rider and can send a wrong signal to the horse, a cue to move forward that you didn't mean. Riding is more about balance than grip."

"Oh."

He showed Cassie how to sit up straight by making an invisible straight line from her ear, down her shoulder, leg and heel. "Now we'll go once around the paddock."

Logan had trained this horse himself, so when he moved, Chocolate did, too. They walked slowly and he was right there, his hand resting on the saddle, ready to grab Cass if she started to slide off. Circuiting the corral was the longest few minutes of his life. And he kept calling out pointers. *Sit up straight. Lower your hands. Don't pull too hard on the reins. Watch where you're going.*

When they got back to where Grace was standing, he

figured that was enough. He'd promised a riding lesson and delivered.

He started to lift her off. "Okay, kiddo. Great job."

"No, Daddy, that wasn't long enough. I want to ride more."

Logan sighed. He didn't have the heart to end it before she was ready, and from the smug look on Grace's face, this scenario wasn't a surprise to her. She'd been counting on it when she got him to agree to a lesson. So, for the next hour he walked his daughter around and around while she chattered away. Over and over she thanked him and said how much she loved Chocolate.

Logan didn't have a lot of good childhood memories, but one of the best was the first time his grandfather put him on a horse and took him riding. His butt hurt, but seeing the land that had been in his family for generations was worth the discomfort. He'd felt connected to something in a deeply profound way. And as he looked at the happiness on his child's face, he wondered if he'd worn the same joyful expression during his first riding lesson.

Grace was leaning against the fence, watching the whole experience, and looked pleased with what was going on. Logan liked that a whole lot better than disappointment. Most of all, he was glad she hadn't quit, and not just because of child care.

"Daddy, I wanna make Chocolate go fast."

Logan hadn't realized the horse shifted a few feet away. When Cassie called out, she pulled his attention back but not in time. She'd lifted her hands holding the reins and yanked the bit in the horse's mouth. He danced sideways unexpectedly, and Cassie slid off to the side. There was a sickening thump just before she cried out.

He rushed to her, and Grace was right behind him. "Cassie?"

She was holding her arm and crying. "Daddy—"

"Baby, you're okay." But he was afraid to touch her.

Oh, God, this was his worst nightmare. He'd wanted more than anything to be wrong, but he wasn't. As expected, she'd gotten hurt because of him.

Logan forced himself to drive the speed limit from the ranch into town. He was taking Cassie to the medical clinic where his sister worked as a nurse practitioner. In the corral, Grace had calmed the little girl down, but she wouldn't let either of them check out her arm. No one except Aunt Jamie could look at it. So he'd scooped her up and put her in the truck.

Now the three of them were moving at what felt somewhere in the neighborhood of slow as molasses. He desperately wanted to put the pedal to the metal, but he kept glancing at the rear seat, where Grace was buckled in beside Cassie's car seat.

"How are you, baby girl?"

"Okay." There were tears in her voice.

"How's the arm?"

"Sore."

"Can you move it?" he asked for the umpteenth time.

"I don't want to." The tone was just south of another meltdown. "It will hurt if I do."

"You don't have to, sweetie." Grace's voice was gentle and calm. "I'm sure it's fine, but your aunt Jamie can tell us for sure. Your daddy will have you at the clinic in no time. He's doing such a great job of driving safely."

For a brief moment, Logan met her gaze in the rearview mirror. That was her way of letting him know that she understood what it was costing him not to drive like a bat out of hell.

"Another few minutes," he said. "I called and Aunt Jamie will be waiting for us."

"Okay."

It was five minutes but felt like five years before he pulled into the Mercy Medical Clinic parking lot. After turning off the truck, he got out and opened the passenger door. Grace had already released the car seat restraints and he lifted Cassie out, taking care not to jostle her injured arm. They headed for the clinic entrance, and his sister was true to her word.

"Hi, sweetheart," she said to her niece. "Come with me."

Logan barely noticed the waiting room. He just concentrated on the back of his sister's blue scrubs as he followed her down a brightly lit hallway with shiny linoleum floors and into an exam room. He started to lower her gently to the paper-covered table, but she resisted.

"No, Daddy. Don't put me down."

"You sit on the table, Logan," Jamie said. "Just hold her on your lap."

He did as instructed. "Okay."

"I need to look at your arm, honey. Can you be brave for me?"

Cassie's bottom lip quivered, but she nodded. "Yes."

Jamie gently took her little arm and straightened it. "Does that hurt?"

"Not much."

"It's scraped, but we'll clean that up." She probed carefully, checking out the shoulder, elbow, wrist and all the areas in between. "Where does it hurt, honey?"

"All over." She sniffled.

Jamie looked at him. "I don't see swelling or anything obvious, but there could be a hairline fracture. The only way to know for sure is to x-ray it. And I know it will drive you nuts if there's any doubt."

"Will it hurt?" Cassie asked. "I don't like shots."

"I don't either," Jamie told her. "X-rays are just pictures of the bone in your arm. It won't hurt. I promise."

"Okay."

"I'll take her to Radiology," Jamie said. "A few years ago we'd have sent you to the hospital an hour away, but the clinic is much better equipped now. And we're not that busy today, so it won't take too long. Why don't you wait here?"

"Is that okay with you, Cass?" he asked her.

"Yes. Aunt Jamie will take good care of me."

"The best," she confirmed. "Sit tight, honey. I'm going to get a special chair for you." She left the room and was back moments later with a children's-sized wheelchair. "Your coach awaits, Princess."

Logan stood with her in his arms and set her carefully on the seat. "Grace and I will wait right here for you, baby girl."

"Okay, Daddy."

"Back in a jiffy," Jamie said.

Logan stared at the doorway after his daughter was wheeled away and kicked himself six ways to Sunday. "This is all my fault."

"Define *this*." Grace was sitting in a visitor's chair against the wall.

"This. Being here." He indicated the medical exam room. "She fell off a horse because of me."

"First of all, your sister didn't seem all that concerned after looking at Cassie's arm."

Logan started pacing. "She's taking an X-ray."

"I sensed that was more about putting your mind at ease." Grace crossed one slender leg over the other. "I was watching her face when Jamie flexed her arm. Not even a flicker of discomfort."

"But she fell off the horse. That's on me," he insisted.

"I would think that a fall comes with the territory when you're learning to ride. Hence the saying that if you fall off a horse you have to get right back on." But there was a guilty expression on her face. "And if anyone is to blame for this, it's me."

"Why? You didn't push her off the horse."

"Neither did you. But I pushed you into putting her on it in the first place. You probably should fire me after all. I wouldn't blame you if you did."

That was like a bucket of cold water over his head. Fire her? As she'd pointed out, if she left he would be on his own. "So you think it was wrong to teach her to ride?"

"No." Her tone was emphatic. "I stand by what I said. That doesn't mean I don't feel awful about her falling. It breaks my heart when she cries."

"I know what you mean. But the buck stops with me. I'm her father. I made the call. My bad."

Grace stood and put herself right in his path, stopping him from pacing. "You're not wrong and you're not bad, Logan."

"And you're too nice—"

"No, I'm not." She looked kind of fierce and ticked off. "Quit being a martyr."

"What?"

"You can't take responsibility for every little thing that goes wrong in Cassie's life. Your job is to let her try new experiences. Of course stuff will happen, but there's a lesson to learn from it, too. You deal when things don't go right."

"But I looked away for a few seconds. I wasn't right there."

"The older she gets, the more that's going to happen. If you don't give her independence at appropriate intervals, she's not going to be prepared when she's an adult." Grace looked up at him, so earnest, so damn pretty.

"I just want to protect her." This was familiar territory, and Grace was well aware. But it was all he had.

"Trying to protect her from everything puts expectations on yourself that are impossible to live up to. It also gives Cassie an unrealistic view of the world. When she was learning to walk, I'm sure she fell down. Did you stop her from walking? Of course not. That's life. Decisions will come up. You think them through and make the best possible judgment."

"That easy?"

"No one said it's easy. But it's being a dad."

Logan felt the tightness in his chest ease up as she talked, and he could finally breathe again. What she said made a lot of sense. She was so close, and more than anything he wanted to pull her against him. Not being able to made his chest squeeze tight again, for a very different reason.

He blew out a breath. "So you think I'm being a martyr?"

She smiled sheepishly. "Not on purpose. I know you're just trying to do the right thing. That counts a lot."

"I'm just trying not to mess her up too bad."

"That's every father's prayer. The sentiment should be cross-stitched and hung on your wall. Along with things never to say to your boss if you want to keep your job."

Funny, she didn't feel like his employee right now. She was so much more than that. Way more than he wanted to even admit.

"I've been meaning to talk to you about that," he teased. "You're a little shy about expressing your opinion."

She laughed. "You must have me mixed up with someone else."

Logan smiled, something he never would have believed could happen when he carried his daughter in here just a little while ago. What magic made it possible?

The exam room door opened, and Jamie wheeled his daughter back into the room. The two of them looked as if they'd been laughing, too.

"That was fast." Logan looked at his sister. "Well?"

"I am officially not the favorite person in Radiology today. Squeaky wheel and all that. But I got the test, and the radiologist read it just to get rid of me." She smiled. "Good news. As I thought, there's nothing broken. I've cleaned up her scrapes, as you can tell by the bandage. She's perfectly fine. Other than a flair for the dramatic, which she gets from her father."

"And that flair really takes off when she's overtired," Grace said.

Jamie nodded. "I see you've met both my brother and my niece."

"You mean the world-famous horseback rider?" Grace teased.

"Daddy!" Cassie's eyes widened, a sign that she'd just thought of something. "I have to talk to Chocolate. Right now."

"He's the horse," Logan told his sister. "Why do you need to talk to him?"

"He might feel bad for makin' me fall off. I need to let him know I'm okay." She got a look on her face, and he wasn't going to like the next words out of her mouth. "Maybe he needs me to ride him again, so he knows for sure he didn't hurt me."

"Simmer down, little cowgirl," Jamie said. "You should probably take it easy for the rest of the day. You're fine this time, but accidents do happen and you're more likely to get hurt if you're overtired."

Logan gave his sister a look that said he owed her big-time. "That sounds like very good medical advice."

"Because I'm a very good medical professional."

Cassie thought that over. "Okay, then, can I ride again tomorrow, Dad?"

Grace squatted down in front of the little girl and brushed strands of loose hair behind her ears. "Why don't we talk about that tomorrow? I bet you're getting hungry."

"How did you know?" Cassie asked.

"Because it happens right about this time every day." Grace looked up at him. "And there's a rumor that the Grizzly Bear Diner has really good hamburgers. I wouldn't know because I've never eaten there. Since it was a job interview, I just had iced tea."

"Daddy, can we take Grace to the diner?"

Logan looked at Grace and the thought went through his mind that he would take her anywhere she wanted. And not just because her dinner suggestion had been the perfect distraction when he really needed it. She just made everything better.

"Grizzly Bear Diner it is." He looked at his sister. "Can you join us?"

She shook her head. "I still have patients. Rain check?"

"You bet. Ladies?"

Cassie hopped out of the wheelchair. "Let's go."

After a hug from her aunt, the little girl took Grace's hand and they walked down the hallway to the front door. Logan followed, thinking about the woman who'd come into his life. She badgered and threatened to convince him to teach his daughter to ride a horse, and he'd learned something, too. Hold the reins a little looser.

He had a feeling he wouldn't have gotten through today without Grace. Lessons were all well and good, but needing her did not make him happy.

Chapter Twelve

Grace was racking her brain to come up with an afternoon activity for Cassie. Her attempt to set up a playdate hadn't worked out because Emily and Paige had other plans, and all the usual activities were considered boring. After being on a horse the day before and having her father's undivided attention, everything suffered by comparison.

"We could do some baking," Grace suggested. "Chocolate chip cookies."

If possible the little girl looked even more down. She was sitting on a high bar stool at the kitchen island and had her chin resting on her folded arms. "I wonder what Chocolate is doin' today."

Oops, Grace thought. She hadn't thought that through. "Maybe some blueberry muffins?"

Cassie shrugged. "I guess."

"Okay. Muffins it is." She'd never realized before how exhausting fake enthusiasm could be. "Let's get out everything we'll need."

She got a mixing bowl from a lower cupboard, then found measuring cups and spoons. Opening the pantry, she poked around for the flour. "I know it's in here somewhere."

The kitchen door opened and closed, and Cassie said, "Daddy!"

"Hi, baby girl."

Grace straightened and turned. She should be used to the way her stomach dropped to her toes every time she saw Logan, but no. The strong jaw, straight nose and blue eyes were something special, and the way he smiled at his little girl just made her heart want to burst.

He looked at her and the baking stuff on the island. "Am I interrupting something?"

"We're going to make blueberry muffins because Miss Cassie is bored and nothing else I suggested appealed to her sense of adventure."

"No tea party?" He was standing beside Cassie and removed his Stetson, then dragged his fingers through his hair.

Even hat hair didn't weaken her acute reaction to him. Why was that? Apparently he just didn't have a bad look. And in a couple of weeks she'd be gone and wouldn't have to see him at all, so that would put an end to her stomach-dropping problem. Funny how that thought didn't produce a whole lot of comfort.

"I didn't feel like having a tea party today," Cassie told him. "There's nothing fun to do."

"Hmm." He settled the hat low on his forehead and frowned. "I'm sorry to hear it. That's a bummer."

The little girl looked up at him with what appeared to be a little like hope in her eyes. "My arm doesn't hurt at all, Daddy."

"Really?"

"This is the first time she's even mentioned it," Grace told him. She'd chattered off and on about the horse and riding but never once brought up the fall or her scraped arm.

"Good."

Something was going on, Grace thought. He almost always came in for lunch, but it was unusual for him to show up at the house in the afternoon. "Is there something you wanted? A snack, maybe?"

"No, I'm good." He looked at her, then his daughter. "I

was just wondering if you're interested in taking a ride on Chocolate this afternoon."

Cassie's mouth dropped open and made on O. "Really?"

"If Grace thinks it's all right."

Of all the things he could have said, that was the most unexpected. "Well—"

"Please say yes, Grace." Cassie's eyes were pleading.

"Your dad is the boss, kiddo. I really don't have any authority on a decision about you and horseback riding."

"But I respect your opinion," he said.

"And I believe you are already aware of what I think. I expressed my views very clearly yesterday at the clinic." She laughed, recalling how he'd teased her about being shy. "I would have thought you remembered."

"I do." His expression turned serious for a moment. "In fact, what you said yesterday is why I'm here right now suggesting it. I'm just checking to see if you had second thoughts."

"If that means you're saying no and I can't ride Chocolate, please don't have second thoughts, Grace."

"You're in luck, Miss Cassie, because I have no such thoughts. I think a ride on Chocolate would be super awesome."

"So, can I, Daddy?"

"Yes," he said.

"Thank you!" She held out her arms to her father. "I'm so happy."

Logan pulled her close and held her for a long time, clearly savoring the hug. And Grace noticed that this time he wasn't the first to let go. Cassie did and started to slide off the stool. Her father intervened and set her on the floor.

"We hafta hurry. Chocolate's waitin' for me."

"Have fun, you two," Grace said. "There will be freshly baked blueberry muffins tonight."

"Aren't you comin'?" Cassie looked at her as if she'd suggested cutting off Princess Aurora's head.

Grace met Logan's gaze as she answered the little girl. "You're in good hands with your dad."

"You hafta come and watch and see how good I do today, Grace."

"Wow, you're really bossy," he teased the little girl. "Not unlike someone else I know."

"I'm not bossy. I just want Grace there, too."

Logan's expression was carefully neutral. "It's okay with me."

The last thing Grace wanted was to intrude on this father/ daughter moment. She'd been pushing for this. "Who's going to cook dinner if I hang out in the corral with you two?"

"Unless you have something complicated planned, why don't we just throw burgers on the grill? Those frozen patties?" he suggested.

"I want a hot dog," Cassie said.

"That would work." He shrugged, and it was impossible to know how he felt when he met her gaze. "Cassie wants you there, so what do you say, Grace?"

"Just so everyone is clear, there won't be fresh blueberry muffins." She waited for someone to object. "All right, then. I wouldn't miss it."

"Yay!" Cassie grabbed her father's big hand in both of hers and tugged. "Let's go."

"Last one to the barn is a rotten egg," he told her.

"Not me." Cassie took off out the back door.

Logan started after her, then glanced over his shoulder. "You coming?"

"Yes."

"Okay." He pulled the door wide and let her precede him.

"You made her so happy, Logan. Did you see her face?" Grace glanced up and saw him smile.

"Yeah. I felt pretty good about that." As they walked down the rocky slope, he grabbed her arm when her heel hit a big stone and made her stumble.

His touch burned like fire, and her stomach clenched. Suddenly it was hard to breathe. For a couple of beats, she was unable to form a coherent response. "You should feel good. I guarantee that this is the right thing to do."

"It feels right." The confidence in his voice was new.

As a teacher, Grace had so many rewarding experiences, but none more than this breakthrough. It was a turning point for him as a father. Proof that he could have a positive influence on his daughter if he let himself get involved. Grace felt a lump in her throat and was glad he didn't say anything else just then that required a response. She couldn't form one. Moments later they walked into the barn, where the little girl was waiting.

"You guys are both rotten eggs." Cassie gave them a triumphant look.

"It's Grace's fault," he said. "She's slow."

"Them's fightin' words. I was just being polite, keeping you company. Next time watch out. No more being nice. I will take you down."

"No way, although I look forward to it," Logan teased back. "I can beat you running backward."

"That I'd like to see—"

"Guys." Cassie's arms were folded over her chest, and there was a stern little look on her face. "You're keeping Chocolate waiting."

"Who knew a horse could be so bossy," Grace said to Logan in a voice only he could hear.

"I noticed." He put his hand on the little girl's shoulder

and steered her to a small room in the barn. "I have a surprise for you."

"What is it, Daddy?"

"If I told you it wouldn't be a surprise." He pointed to a bag on the workbench in the tack room.

Cassie ran over, and her body was quivering with excitement when she pulled a sparkly pink bicycle helmet out of the bag. "For me?"

"Protective head gear," he confirmed. "I made a quick trip into town for it this morning. Every beginning rider should wear one. It's like a crown for the corral."

"I love it. Thank you, Daddy."

"You're welcome, baby girl."

Wow, Grace thought, if Logan kept this up, he would be a hands-down favorite for Father of the Year. "Way to go."

Logan smiled at her praise, then was all business. "Now it's time to saddle up Chocolate."

As he did that, he explained to his daughter everything he was doing and why he was doing it, even though she was too little to handle this herself. Or even remember everything. He was planting seeds, making every moment a teachable one.

Grace would bet everything she was saving for a house that Logan's grandfather had started his training like this. The parental instinct groundwork had been put in place even though he didn't yet realize it. He'd just needed a push to take a leap of faith.

When Chocolate was all set, he looked at his helmeted daughter. "Are you ready?"

"Yes!"

"Okay." He scooped her into his arms and settled her in the saddle, then handed her the reins. "Remember, hold them firmly but don't tug. That's what happened yesterday, and Chocolate got confused and nervous."

"Okay, Daddy."

He walked toward the barn's exit into the corral, and the horse moved with him. In a quiet, reassuring voice he reminded Cassie to sit up straight, let her body go with the animal's movement and learn to feel her balance. He showed her how to signal the horse if she wanted him to go left, right or increase his pace.

"You're doing a great job, Cass." There was parental pride in his expression and his tone. "You're a natural."

"Must be in the genes," Grace commented.

"My legs are in my jeans." Cassie took it literally, making them laugh. She looked indignant. "What's so funny?"

"Grace just meant that you take after me," Logan explained.

"Mommy says I look like you." Cassie kept her eyes straight ahead, watching where she was going as instructed.

"Your mom is right," Grace said. "And I see a lot of your mom's even-tempered personality in you."

"When's Mommy comin' home?"

"Not too much longer." Logan's voice seemed unusually deep.

What did that mean? Grace had been aware that the days were flying by and there was only a short amount of time left on her employment contract. But for some reason the words hit her squarely in the chest, right around her heart. There would be only a few more days like this one. She was here in the corral because Cassie had insisted and Logan had agreed.

She'd been wanted.

The joy of that realization spilled through her before her old friend loneliness pushed it away. The irony didn't escape her. Grace had insisted on yesterday's riding lesson because she couldn't bear the thought of Logan keeping himself cut off from the people he loved. Because she would be leaving soon. She'd tried not to become attached to Cassie and Logan but had failed miserably. So she was the one who would be cut off.

She was going to miss both of them terribly when she went back to Buckskin Pass.

"Mommy's here!" Cassie had been in a flurry of expectation ever since Tracy called to let them know she was back from her trip and would come by late in the afternoon to pick her up. The little girl had been looking out the window for a while now, and the wait was finally over.

Grace glanced at the suitcases sitting in the entryway with all Cass's clothes and toys. She put her hand on the girl's shoulder and watched Tracy get out of the car. The last days had flown by. Heck, the whole summer had passed in a blur of laughter, longing and a feeling of belonging— even if it was only temporary.

"I'm going to answer the door."

Grace was right behind her and looked on as Cassie pulled it wide and greeted her mom. They hugged, laughed and cried.

After a few moments, Tracy brushed the moisture from her cheeks. "Hi, Grace."

"Welcome home. How was your trip?"

"Magical." She stood but settled a hand across her daughter's shoulders, keeping her close. "London. Paris. Rome, Venice and Florence. And to see those stunning places with the love of my life—" Her eyes grew suspiciously moist again. "I don't even have the words to describe how wonderful it was."

"Did you bring me something?" Cassie looked up, excitement lighting her face.

"No. This trip was for me and my new husband—" She started laughing at the child's change of expression. "I can't do it. Of course we brought you something—from every place we went. In fact, we had to buy another suitcase just to bring home all the things we got you."

"I knew you were just kidding." Cassie wrapped her arms around her mother's waist.

"Can't fool you." She met Grace's gaze. "So, how did things go here? Knowing my daughter, she would have said something during our phone calls, but…just checking."

Probably wouldn't be a good idea to share that she'd slept with Logan—especially with Cassie standing right there. Or that, for Grace, nothing had changed. Her attraction hadn't gone away, and he wasn't a handsome jerk. Just the opposite—too caring for his own good.

"Things went really well," she said.

"Mommy—" Cassie tugged on her hand to get her attention "—Daddy's teaching me to ride a horse."

Tracy blinked first at her daughter, then Grace. "Get out."

"It's true. And in the interest of full disclosure, after her very first ride, she fell off."

"But I'm okay, Mom. Daddy took me to see Aunt Jamie, and she took a picture of the bone in my arm. It wasn't broken."

"Thank goodness."

"And the next day, I went riding again!"

"Did you sneak a ride, or was your father around?" Tracy asked skeptically.

"It was actually his suggestion," Grace said. To be fair she'd encouraged him, then stood back and watched. It was a moment she'd never forget. And Cassie wouldn't either.

"Wow. Do you like riding, honey?"

"I love it! It's so much fun."

"She's her father's daughter," Tracy said.

"That she is," Grace agreed. "But I think she got the obsession for tea parties from you."

"Remember I told you, Mommy. Daddy came to one and he played Prince Adam from *Beauty and the Beast*."

"He was a big hit," Grace explained. "You're probably already aware, but there's a deplorable lack of men to play the male leads."

Tracy laughed. "Oh, to be a fly on the wall and see Logan at a tea party. You didn't by any chance take videos?"

"No. YouTube's loss. But I did promise discretion."

"Ah." A gleam of understanding slid into the other woman's eyes. "So you got him there through some kind of magic."

"The word you're looking for is *blackmail*."

"This gets better and better."

"What does *blackmail* mean?" Cassie asked.

The two women exchanged a glance, then Grace thought for a moment. "It means that after a playdate with Emily and Paige when Wendy showed up to retrieve the girls, the words *pick up* took on a whole new meaning."

Tracy nodded her understanding. "Revenge body strikes again. Not to be repetitious, but oh, to be a fly on the wall. What happened?"

Grace took pity on him even though she was annoyed because he'd disappeared emotionally. "There was dedicated flirting, and I may have bailed him out. But he was the one who said he owed me."

Tracy obviously understood that his forfeit was attendance at his daughter's pretend tea party. She looked down at Cassie. "That sounds awesome, sweetheart."

"It was so much fun, Mommy." She looked up, pleading in her eyes. "Can we go home now? I want to see what you brought me."

"Of course we can. But first I want to say hi to your dad

and thank him for taking such good care of you. And you need to tell him goodbye."

"He's in the barn." Cassie headed for the front door. "I need to say goodbye to Chocolate, too."

"That's the horse she's been riding," Grace explained.

"Oh, thank God. I was afraid she meant the candy and somehow that was going to create a challenge for me."

Grace laughed. "I think the name came from his coloring. And other than her little spill, she's really taken to him. He really is a gentle pony."

"Doesn't surprise me. That's exactly what Logan would pick for her." Tracy slid her big sunglasses to the top of her head. "The shocker is how he got talked into putting her on a horse in the first place."

"What do you mean?"

"For quite a while now she's been wanting to ride."

"I figured. The first night I was here he explained she'd be spending a lot of time with me because he had to run the ranch." It was surprising how clearly she recalled the exact conversation even though that night felt like a lifetime ago. And yet it seemed like yesterday, too. "She reminded him he had to teach her to ride."

"So he agreed?" Tracy sounded amazed.

"Not then. It took some convincing."

"Blackmail again? Because I'm fairly sure you had something to do with persuading him."

"Someone had to."

"Mind telling me how you did it?" Tracy folded her arms over her chest.

Since the job was technically over now, there was no reason not to explain. Grace shrugged. "I threatened to quit."

The other woman's eyes went wide. "Bold move."

"It was something I felt very strongly about." For a lot of reasons.

Some of them were about Cassie and the part of Grace's job that had to do with caring for her. But concern for Logan was what had finally made up her mind to go for it. She had to make him see that he was wrong about himself, that he could have a positive impact on his daughter's life. Put a crack in the wall that kept everyone out. Show him that he didn't have to be a loner. Cassie needed him, and almost as important, he needed her.

Tracy was thoughtful for several moments. "I've been trying to talk him into teaching her for months. But I had nothing to bargain with because he doesn't care about me."

"Of course he does," Grace protested. "You're friends. More important, you're the mother of his child."

"That's my point. I can't quit either one of those things. I could have made threats to stop being his friend, but that's only symbolic since we still have to deal with each other regarding Cassie." She shook her head. "Plus, he just doesn't feel *that way* about me."

"What way?"

"I can't believe I have to spell this out for you." The other woman sighed dramatically. "He has the hots for you, Grace. I saw it at the wedding. Everyone could see it."

Grace's cheeks burned with embarrassment, and no doubt the other woman could see that, too. Denying they had the hots for each other would be a lie, what with having sex when they got back here to the ranch. And then there was that night in the kitchen when he came right out and said he wanted her but couldn't touch her because he would hate himself in the morning.

The problem was that passion was one thing and making a life together was something altogether different. That required commitment, and Logan was committed only to being alone.

"I admit there was an attraction," Grace said delicately.

"I knew it." Tracy's look was triumphant. "That's great. I'm so happy for you two."

That made one of them. "There is no 'us two.' It doesn't change anything."

"Maybe it could," the other woman persisted. "You're good for Logan, Grace. Take it from his best friend. He needs someone like you, someone he respects and will listen to."

"Threatening to quit is a lot different from his listening to me."

"The fact that it worked is because he didn't want you to go. That means he cares," Tracy insisted.

"It means he didn't want childcare responsibilities to interfere with him running the ranch. He has very specific ideas about where it's safe for her. So darn obstinate—"

"And there's another reason why I think you'd be perfect for him." Tracy looked exasperated.

"I'm sorry. That one went right over my head."

"You're just as stubborn as he is."

"I take that as a compliment." Grace laughed.

"Good, because that's the way I meant it." Tracy sighed. "I just wish you'd think about it."

Grace had thought about little else since meeting Logan, but that hadn't gotten her very far. Even if she wanted her and Logan to be an "us," it wasn't a smart move.

"You're sweet to say so, Tracy."

"Okay. Message received. Thanks for indulging me." The other woman nodded. "And now I'll mind my own business. My only excuse for sticking my nose in is jet lag. And I care a lot about Logan."

Grace cared, too. So much that part of her was tempted to believe he did need her and still had the hots for her. The truth was that if he touched her, kissed her, she would be his for the taking.

So it was a good thing she had to spend only one more night under his roof. The drive back to Buckskin Pass was kind of long, and he'd agreed that she should tackle it first thing in the morning. Tonight she would put her belongings in suitcases, but she didn't need anything to carry her feelings in. There was a reason emotional leftovers were called baggage.

Her tenderness toward Logan would come with her when she went back where she came from. She refused to call it home. Not until she had roots, and that meant a house with her name on the title. Thanks to this job she now had the money to make that happen.

Maybe someday it would be enough.

Chapter Thirteen

"Daddy, Chocolate is gonna miss me when I go back to Mommy's."

Logan had walked his daughter and her mom back up to the house. He glanced at Tracy, who was pressing her lips together to hide a grin. "I'm sure he will miss you, baby girl. I know I will."

"What if I forget how to ride?" she asked.

So that's where she was going with this, he thought. If not for all these weeks with his daughter, it would have taken him a lot longer to figure out she wasn't so much worried about missing the horse as she was not being able to ride him again.

"You won't forget, honey. It's like driving a car," he assured her.

The little girl looked up at him. "But I don't know how to drive a car."

Logan ignored Tracy's snort of laughter. "I just meant that everything you learned will stick with you. Especially because your mom and I are going to work something out so you can come over and ride all the time. Chocolate is going to see you so much he'll take one look at you and say, 'Not her again.'"

"No, he won't. He can't talk." She giggled. "I'm gonna tell Grace."

Logan watched her run into the house and thought about Grace. She was leaving for good, and he hated the thought of saying goodbye. "I guess you can see for yourself that Grace did a great job with Cassie while you were away."

"Yeah. The little stinker probably didn't even know I was gone."

"She noticed, believe me. But Grace stepped in seamlessly." He glanced at the house. "Cassie's really going to miss her."

"Is she the only one?"

Logan's gaze snapped back to hers. "What?"

"You heard me." She leaned back against the hood of her SUV. "I think you're going to miss Grace as much, if not more, than your daughter."

He was trying not to think about life after Grace. More than that he really didn't want to talk about this. "I just wanted you to know she did a good job. In case you were wondering."

"First of all, I knew that. She's the one who convinced you to let Cassie ride. Second—" she paused dramatically "—this is me. I know you're not this dense."

In his opinion, one of Tracy's best qualities was her determination. It was also her worst. When she took a bite out of something, it was next to impossible to get her to let go. She was right. He knew exactly where she was going with this.

"Just leave it alone, Trace."

There was regret in her eyes. "You're different since Grace."

"Nope." He looked down at his scuffed and dusty boots, his old comfortable jeans. What wasn't comfortable was this conversation. "I'm the same."

"You're deliberately misunderstanding. I mean with Cassie. You're different." She folded her arms over her chest. "I don't know how to explain it, but you have a bond with your daughter that wasn't there before."

"You're imagining things." He pushed back, but the truth was he did feel closer to Cass.

"No." Tracy shook her head. "It's like some invisible wall inside you has disappeared. You're more at ease with her. More accessible. Not holding back."

"I think it's just that you've been away for a while," he said. "And this is the longest stretch of time she's spent with me."

"No. It's more than that. This is because of Grace."

"How could you possibly know that? You've been back for what? Fifteen seconds?"

Tracy just smiled at his outburst, as if she knew some secret handshake. "You forget how well I know you."

"Apparently not well enough since you're wrong about this."

"I had a chat with Grace before Cassie and I met you in the barn. I know you taught your daughter to ride because she threatened to quit. It worked because you were more terrified of losing Grace and being alone with your child than you were of putting her on a horse."

Women had an annoying way of talking about everything, he thought. Good, bad, ugly, it didn't matter. They talked and bonded. They spilled it all. There was a good chance she also knew Grace maneuvered him into that tea party, too. But the memory made him smile. The happy little girl who hugged him hard that night. It was something he would never forget.

"We had some good times," was all he said.

"Thanks in no small part to Grace." Tracy studied him. "She made a difference."

Logan chose to believe the difference she meant was his relationship with his daughter. "Cassie really took to her."

"I think you did, too. And why not? She's fabulous." Tracy was dead serious.

He waited for her to blister his ears with what she thought about him sleeping with Grace, an employee. But she just stared at him, which meant not quite *everything* between the women had been shared. Then her words completely sank in. She believed he'd taken to Grace. Personally.

"She's got a way about her," he admitted.

"I knew it!" Tracy straightened away from the car and hugged him. "She's good for you, Logan."

"No point in debating whether or not that's true. She's leaving tomorrow."

"Does she have to?"

"Yeah. She's got a life in Buckskin Pass."

"She's a teacher. School doesn't start for a couple of weeks." She gave him a sharp look. "You do the math."

More time with Grace. That thought shot adrenaline straight through him. They did have fun together. But she had work and a life somewhere else, so it was inevitable that she would go. Still, because of that time limit there was no danger of him doing her long-term damage. And what if…

He smiled at Tracy. "Have I ever told you that you're a major pain in the neck?"

"It's why you love me like a brother."

"Says who?"

"Enough said." She laughed. "Seriously, though, we will have to work out a schedule for Cassie to ride. I can bring her out here. You could pick her up."

"If ranch work runs late or something, we can ride and she can spend the night. I'll take her to school," he offered.

"The connection to this land and the animals is in her blood. She is her father's daughter."

"That's what Grace said."

Tracy's expression clearly said "I told you so."

"She's a very special woman."

The front door opened, and Cassie came running out,

followed by Grace. "I forgot this stuff," she said, holding up a bag. "Grace found my bedtime bear and my favorite book."

"Thank you, Grace." Tracy hugged her. "You may have just saved one of us an emergency trip."

"Happy to help."

"I'm hungry." The little girl handed the bag to her mom. "Grace is makin' mac and cheese. It's my favorite."

"Your daughter is not subtle." Grace laughed. "But I made plenty. Would you like to stay for dinner?"

"Tempting," Tracy said. "But my husband is waiting."

"Wow, husband." Logan was sincerely happy for her.

"I know. The glow of it all hasn't worn off yet."

"Something tells me it never will." Grace looked wistful. "If you'd like, I can put some in a container and send it home with you."

"That would be fantastic."

"It will just take a minute." Grace went back inside. It didn't take her long to return with a large, covered plastic bowl filled with creamy macaroni. "Here you go."

Tracy took the container. "Thanks for this. And for taking such good care of my daughter."

"She's a joy." There was complete honesty in her voice.

Logan had seen with his own eyes that she'd treated his child like her own.

"Will I ever see you again, Grace?" Cassie looked up, tears in her eyes. "I'm sad that you're going back home."

He knew exactly how she felt, which made comforting words hard to come by.

"Maybe you can come and visit me," Grace suggested. "And we can talk on the phone."

"It won't be the same." The little girl held her arms out, and Grace went down on one knee to embrace her. "I love you."

"I love you, too, sweetie…" Her voice broke. After a few moments she pulled away.

"We have to go, Cass. Bye, Grace. Logan said you're leaving first thing in the morning. Have a safe trip home."

He didn't miss the subtext of the look Tracy slid to him. The one that said "don't be an idiot." Every day he did his best not to be, but sometimes he didn't know how to prevent it.

He and Grace stood side by side watching the car drive away. When it rounded a curve and disappeared from sight, he said, "You made mac and cheese for dinner?"

"And fried chicken. Biscuits, too. Pure comfort food." She sighed a little sadly. "I don't know about you, but I'm feeling it was a good call." Without another word, she turned and went inside.

Logan followed her into the kitchen and washed his hands at the sink. "Is there anything I can do?"

"Goodbye is just a fact of life." She forced a perky tone into her voice that didn't match the dejection in her expression.

"Actually, I meant can I do anything to help with dinner?"

"Oh." She thought for a moment. "You can set the table while I make a salad."

"Okay."

Logan did as instructed and had mixed feelings looking at the two places he'd set at the table instead of three. He would miss Cassie. Her cheerful chatter. Her laughter. The nighttime ritual of putting her to bed. When he let himself be a part of it, this had felt like a family. A traditional, normal family. On the other hand, he was going to be alone with Grace. The prospect had heat pooling in his belly.

"Would you like a glass of wine?"

Her hands stilled as she met his gaze. "I am off the clock, so…yes."

"I'll open it." He popped the cork on a chilled bottle of Chardonnay and poured some into two glasses, then set them on the table.

Grace finished the salad and set it out before adding the platter of chicken, a casserole dish filled with pasta and a basket of biscuits. "All set."

"Smells great." He waited for her to sit down, then took his place. "I'm starved."

"I made plenty so there will be leftovers. You won't have to cook for a couple of days after I'm gone." She took a sip of wine and looked at him. "After dinner I have to pack."

He missed most of what she said after *gone.* The word echoed through him, a reminder of how much emptier the house would be this time tomorrow. Grace would be back in Buckskin Pass and he would be eating leftovers by himself.

He stared hard at her sweet, pretty face, and an ache settled in his chest. Tracy's words were fresh in his mind, and she was right. Maybe it was possible to have just a little bit longer. "You could stay."

"What?" There was surprise and something that looked a lot like hope in her eyes.

"When do you have to go back to teaching?"

"Two weeks. The staff goes back for meetings and to get classrooms ready for the kids."

"So, technically you're on vacation," he clarified.

"Yes."

"Then stay here a little longer." *With me,* he almost said. But asking her to stay was already a step more than he was completely comfortable with. He chalked it up to the power of Grace.

A slow smile curved up the corners of her full lips. "I guess I can put off the packing for a bit."

Logan felt like a condemned man getting a last-minute reprieve. Relief flooded through him, and he smiled back. "Okay, then."

"That's a classic example of show, don't tell." She was looking at him expectantly.

"I'm not sure what you mean."

"You are strong, responsible and protective, Logan. The personification of a rugged individualist."

"Is that your way of saying I'm a man of action?" He couldn't help grinning at her.

"Yes," she agreed. "Asking me to stay is the cowboy way of saying you care."

Maybe more than he should. "I'm not great with flowery speeches."

"I noticed." She nodded. "And it's okay. I love you, too."

Before he could figure out how to respond to that, Grace changed the subject. If he was being honest with himself, that was almost as much of a relief as not having to tell her goodbye yet. He didn't know what to say. It's not like he hadn't been completely honest. He'd told her he didn't do love.

So her declaration was probably not as complicated as he was making it out to be. More that she was looking forward to staying just a little longer. Because they had fun together.

Okay, he thought. Weirdness avoided. Now he could just look forward to the time he would have alone with her.

Grace had just started the coffee when Logan walked in the back door. At oh-dark-thirty that morning, he'd kissed her and slipped out of bed to go feed the stock. The same as the last few mornings since he'd asked her to stay. And she'd spent those magical nights in his bed. After chores he came back to the house for breakfast with her.

"Hey, cowboy, are you hungry?"

A teasing look slid into his blue eyes as he walked over and pulled her close to his lean body. "Hungry for you."

"But you just had me last night." Memories of what they'd done made her shiver, and heat crept into her cheeks.

The truth was they'd had each other every night and couldn't seem to get enough. It was clear to Grace that she fell more deeply in love with him every day. The only cloud in her sky was that he hadn't said how he felt. She was all for show, don't tell, but at some point a girl needed to hear the words. Because she couldn't forget Logan's warning not to fall for him. It hadn't done any good.

He kissed her, just a soft, sweet touch of his lips to hers. Then he looked at her with a wicked gleam in his eyes. "I intend to have you tonight, too. Any objections?"

"I can't think of a single one." She batted her eyes at him. "But when you kiss me like that I can't think at all."

"I promise to use my powers only for good," he said solemnly. But the twinkle in his eyes was the cutest thing ever.

"You won't disappoint me?"

"No."

"All right, then. I'll cook you a meal that won't disappoint you either."

"Then you must have made blueberry muffins. And omelets are in my future. I know you well."

"You're right about the menu," she said. "As far as knowing me well? I'm not buying it. The smell of freshly baked muffins is in the air, not to mention they're right there on the cooling rack."

"But there's no evidence of omelets, so a guy can hope. I just really like them."

"How can I resist sweet talk like that?"

She smiled happily, wearing her heart on her sleeve. It was impossible to resist the feelings, and once she'd recognized that she loved him, she didn't want to fight them anymore. She had decided to enjoy every moment with him and see what happened.

The eggs didn't take long. She put out a bowl of fresh strawberries and slid an omelet onto each of their plates. They sat at the table across from each other and started to eat.

Logan split a muffin in half, then buttered it and took a bite. "Mmm. This is the best."

"I'm glad you like them. In fact, I'm beginning to think that's the only reason you asked me to stay."

"Not the only reason."

"You enjoy my witty conversation?"

He nodded. "You're a talker for sure."

"So," she said, "cooking and talking made the top ten. What else?"

"I like waking up with you." His voice lowered into the seductive range.

Grace felt tingles two-step up and down her spine. "Anything else?"

"You're a pretty good kisser."

"Good to know you think I have skills beyond just cooking."

"Now you're just fishing for compliments," he teased.

"I thought you didn't notice."

"There's nothing about you I don't notice." His eyes flashed with intensity before he smiled. "Can you ride a horse?"

"I've been on one, but you were right about my learning everything I know from watching Westerns. Why?"

"I'd like to show you the ranch on horseback."

Grace knew how much the land meant to him, so the simple words felt intimate and massaged her heart in all the right places. "I'd love to see it."

"Okay, then."

There was more teasing small talk while they finished breakfast then lingered over another cup of coffee. This was the perfect way to start the day, she thought. Sitting across from a handsome, thoughtful man who appreciated her cooking and noticed everything about her.

He finished the last of his coffee. "I'll saddle a couple of horses for us."

"While you do that," she said, "I'll clean up the dishes."

"I can stay and help," he offered.

"That's okay. I'll just meet you in the barn when I'm finished."

"Okay." He stood and carried his plate to the sink.

Grace followed and put her dishes on top of his. "I'll see you in a few minutes."

"I'll be waiting." He cupped her face in his hands and kissed her. "Don't be long."

Too breathless to speak, Grace simply nodded. When he was gone, she rinsed the plates and utensils, then put them in the dishwasher. She stored the leftover muffins in a plastic container and washed all the pans and bowls used for cooking. Glancing around, she made sure that everything was in order. Satisfied, she was just about to head out when the doorbell rang.

"Logan?" she said to herself. Wouldn't he just come in?

A vaguely uneasy sensation trickled through her as she went to answer the front door. When she did, Foster Hart was standing there.

"Hello, Grace."

"Mr. Hart. This is a surprise."

"I was in the area. My apologies for stopping by without warning, but you saw for yourself that Logan is resistant to my overtures."

"Yes, I did. And he told me why. Can you blame him?"

"No." The regret in his expression looked genuine. "Would you mind if I came in?"

"Logan isn't here."

He looked disappointed. "Would it be all right if you and I talk?"

Grace was conflicted. She understood better than most why Logan wanted nothing to do with his father. But what if the man sincerely wanted to make amends?

"All right," she said, pulling the door wider. "Can I get you a cup of coffee?"

"Yes. Thank you." He followed her into the kitchen.

Grace got out a mug and poured leftover coffee into it. Since she'd just turned off the heat under the pot, the dark liquid was still warm. "Cream? Sugar?"

"Black is fine." He took the mug from her.

"What is it you want to talk about?"

"Cassie." There was a tone in his voice that sounded a lot like yearning. "I talked to Tracy. She's open to my getting to know my granddaughter but said the final decision is Logan's."

"I see." Grace studied the man. There was silver at his temples, and he was fit and tan. Handsome. She could see a lot of Logan in him. A preview of how he would look when he got older. "Surely you can understand that Logan doesn't trust you not to hurt Cassie."

Foster sighed. "I've made a lot of mistakes. I know that. I drove Logan's mother away and my children, too. I deeply regret what I did to them. Does he know that I tried to give her money but she flatly refused any help from me?"

"I don't think so." Grace was pretty sure he would have told her.

"She turned to her father, and I understand why. But I'm not the complete bastard my son believes. I wouldn't knowingly abandon my family or let them live without a roof over their heads."

"I don't know what to say, Mr. Hart. Logan's feelings are deeply entrenched."

"Doesn't everyone deserve a second chance?"

Grace thought so. If her father and mother asked forgiveness and to be a part of her life, she would gladly make room. But she wasn't Logan. In all fairness, her parents had given her away, and she hoped it was because they believed she would have a better life than they could give her. She wasn't dealing with a pattern of betrayal.

"Look, Mr. Hart, this is something you should talk to Logan about."

"According to Tracy, you've been good for him. I was hoping you could put in a word for me."

There were footsteps behind her, and Logan said, "Here are two words. *Get out.*"

Grace's stomach dropped. She turned and nearly flinched at the fury burning in his eyes. "Maybe you should hear him out."

"That's not going to happen."

"I apologize, son, for what I did to you. I would very much appreciate a chance to show you I've changed. If you could see your way to letting me know Cassie and for her to know me—"

"No." Logan was abrupt and emphatic. "I don't believe you're capable of changing, and there's no way I'll risk you hurting my child the way you did yours."

"Son—"

"Don't call me that."

Foster stared at him for several moments, then resignation settled on his face, making him look older, defeated. He set his untouched mug on the counter beside him. "All

right. I'll go. Grace, thank you for the coffee. And for listening. Goodbye."

The man walked out of the room, and moments later the
front door closed. Instead of relief that he was gone, Grace
felt the tension between her and Logan grow.

He looked ready to snap. "I came to check on you when
you didn't show up."

"I figured."

"You shouldn't have let him in." He was accusing her
of something. Colluding with the enemy?

"Did you know he tried to give your mother money?"

"That's his story."

"What if it's true?"

"I'd say he didn't try hard enough to help her."

"Logan, he's older now. They say there's a little bit of
wrong on the other side of right. That means there's a little bit of right on the other side of wrong. Maybe he has
regrets and would like to try to make up for what he did.
Maybe he's not all bad."

"He's bad enough." He drew back as if burned when she
put her hand on his arm. "There's too much of that man in
me. I can't do this, Grace."

"What are you saying? You're asking me to leave?"

The anger in his eyes receded for a moment, letting pain
show. Then he said, "It would be best for you."

"Don't do this, Logan."

"I should never have asked you to stay. My bad."

"You say that a lot. Too much. You're not bad," she said,
willing him to believe her. "This is about protecting yourself from being hurt."

"See? It's all about me." He smiled, but there was no
humor in it. "Just like him. Selfish."

"No. That's not what I meant and not who you are."

"You're wrong." His tone left no room for further argument.

She looked him straight in the eyes and said, "No, you're wrong. I wish you could see yourself the way everyone else sees you. The way *I* see you. You're a good and decent man, and it makes me sad that you're turning your back on what could be a wonderful thing between us."

"I'm not a good bet. Forget about me, Grace."

Yeah, fat chance of that. "All right. I'll go, but I hope you'll change your mind about us. And I can't guarantee for how long, but I'll wait for you. ."

"Don't. Please don't. I don't want to hurt you. Not ever."

"Too late."

She left him standing in the kitchen and went upstairs to pack her things. It was hard to hold back tears, but she managed. The problem was, if she let go she wouldn't be able to stop.

The day had started out like heaven, and it took only a few minutes with Foster Hart to send it to hell. So much for Logan having her tonight. And so much for not disappointing her. Worst of all, he believed he was doing it *for* her.

This job had given her the money to buy a house and put one man's betrayal behind her. Now she knew there were a whole lot of ways to let someone down. Taking her money hurt much less than being soul-deep in love with a man who wouldn't love her back.

Chapter Fourteen

It was stupid that he missed Grace more when Cassie was with him at the ranch, but when had he ever been smart where Mary Poppins was concerned? Logan had gotten used to the three of them being together, and it felt as if one of the musketeers had skipped town.

Tracy had brought the little girl out every day to ride, but now it was the weekend and she'd be spending the night for the first time since Grace had gone home to Buckskin Pass. Instead of the mall or a movie, they were in the corral, and she was trotting Chocolate around as if she'd been born in the saddle.

If not for Grace, Logan probably wouldn't be having this particular moment. Instead of thanking her, he'd sent her packing. The decision was knee-jerk, but he shouldn't still be second-guessing it. She was always going to leave anyway. He'd simply cut the ties a little sooner. But the fact was he felt like pond scum. And the damn empty feeling inside him wouldn't go away.

"Look at me, Daddy!"

"I'm watching, baby girl." That wasn't exactly a lie. He'd just been thinking hard about Grace's sweet smile while he did.

"Am I doing okay?" She moved the reins, giving the horse a cue.

When Chocolate walked over and stopped in front of

him, Logan patted the horse's neck. "You're doing great, kiddo."

"Grace would be really happy I'm doing so good."

"She would."

"I wish she could see me."

Logan wished he could see *her*, just standing by the fence, smiling at him as if he were her star pupil. "I can't believe how fast you're learning."

"Can I go outside the corral?" She gave him that pleading look. The one that said she knew he wouldn't like it but would he please just say yes.

"We'll take a ride to the lake."

Logan wasn't prepared for the sudden, unexpected stab of longing that cut through him. That's the trail he'd wanted to show Grace the day his father dropped in unexpectedly. Claiming he wanted a chance to know his granddaughter.

"Oh, boy! The lake." Cassie was quivering with excitement. "Can we go now?"

"It's almost dinnertime. And the sun is getting pretty low in the sky. We'd run out of light, and it can be dangerous to ride in the dark. If the horse puts his foot wrong, he could injure himself. And you."

"I wouldn't want Chocolate to get hurt."

"Of course you wouldn't."

"Grace says we should be kind to all living things. Even bugs," Cassie said seriously.

That sounded like Grace. She was beautiful inside and out. The truth was, Logan hadn't been very kind to her. He'd refused to listen to anything about his father. But thinking about it later had tweaked his curiosity. He'd asked his brother if he remembered anything about their mother refusing money or help from Foster Hart. Turned out Tucker did recall that.

It seemed her pride had kicked in because she loved

him so much and didn't want him to see her as pitiful. His brother also recalled their father showing up at the ranch and Granddad running him off to protect them.

Since finding out all this, Logan had been questioning his decisions regarding his father. He'd talked with Tracy about introducing him to Cassie. Like Grace, she believed the man sincerely regretted what he'd done to his family. She also thought it unfair to deprive their daughter of the opportunity to meet her grandfather and form her own opinion.

Two months ago if anyone had told him he would even consider this, he'd have said they were nuts. But the really crazy thing was that it didn't feel wrong. Still more of Grace's influence on his life.

"Hey, kiddo, we need to curry Chocolate and feed him before I feed you."

"Okay."

Logan lifted her off the horse's back when she held out her arms to him. He squeezed her close, feeling love well up inside him that pushed out everything bad for a few moments. Normally she wiggled to get down, but for some reason she hugged him tight. Maybe feeling a little insecure and clingy. Maybe missing Grace. Maybe she sensed he needed it.

"I love you, Daddy."

"Love you, too, Cass." He put her down. "Do you want to lead Chocolate into his stall?"

Her eyes grew wide because she'd been asking to do this and so far he'd said no. Until now. "Can I?"

He handed her the reins. "Go for it."

"Come on, Chocolate." She headed for the barn entrance, and the horse obediently followed. "Oh, boy. Grace would be so excited to see me doin' this. Wouldn't she, Daddy?"

"You bet she would." He could picture the pleased smile on her face and just a hint of I-told-you-so in her eyes.

After walking the horse into his hay-covered stall, Cassie handed back the reins. "I'll go get the curry brush."

"Okay. Good job."

While teaching her to ride, he'd also been impressing on her the obligation of taking good care of the animals. She was a natural and soaking it all up like a sponge. Logan secured the horse by wrapping the reins around a fence slat. Then he unbuckled the cinch beneath the horse's belly and lifted off the saddle before setting it on top of the stall fence.

Cassie returned and held out the brush. "Here, Daddy."

"Why don't you give it a try?"

"I can't reach."

"Do the parts you can and I'll get the rest," he said.

"Okay." She beamed with confidence.

Logan watched carefully as she slid the brush onto her little hand and moved it over Chocolate's lower body and the part of the mane at her level. There was fierce concentration on her little face as she performed the task. He was so proud of her. It occurred to him that this was another father/daughter moment he wouldn't have if not for Grace.

"Daddy." Cassie looked up a little sadly. "Grace never got to see me do this."

"I know."

"She would have liked watchin' me."

"Yeah." Apparently he wasn't the only one thinking about her. "Do you want me to take over, baby girl?"

"Okay." She handed him the brush and supervised, pointing out places he'd missed. "Don't forget his mane, Daddy."

"You've been taking notes."

"Huh?" She stared blankly at him.

He grinned. "I just meant you've been paying attention to what I've been saying."

"I'm practicin' payin' attention for kindergarten. Grace said it's important to listen when the teacher's talkin'."

"She would know all about that."

If her impact on his daughter was anything to go by, the kids she taught were really lucky to have her. And those kids lived in Buckskin Pass, a three-hour drive from Blackwater Lake. The empty feeling came back with a vengeance, and he wanted to believe it was only because he was hungry.

"I think Chocolate is groomed just fine. What do you think, Cass?"

"Good job, Daddy."

"Okay. What do you say we go eat?"

"I'm starvin'."

Logan removed the bit from the horse's mouth, secured the gate, then hung up the tack. Side by side, he and Cassie walked up to the house. For the last week he hadn't looked forward to going inside when the place was so quiet. At least for the weekend his daughter was there, so it wouldn't feel quite so empty.

He was grateful to Grace for pushing him to bond with his child but not the part where he felt so much lonelier than he had before he knew her. If they'd never met, he wouldn't know what missing her was like. But he couldn't undo meeting her, so there was no choice but to appreciate the good and gut it out with the bad. He'd get over it. He'd get over *her*.

After both of them had washed up, Logan poured frozen fries on a cookie sheet, then put it in the oven to heat. After that he turned on the grill just outside the kitchen door and cooked the hot dogs. Cassie had insisted Grace always let her set the table, so she handled that after he got plates down from the cupboard.

When he set the platter containing grilled hot dogs on the table, his daughter turned up her nose. "They're burned. I don't like the black part. Grace never did it like that."

Logan needed patience and he needed it now. It wasn't so much the critique of his grilling style as much as it was her constantly talking about Grace. Thoughts of her kept popping into his mind anyway, but with Cassie reminding him of everything, he didn't get a break from the feelings. Every time he heard her name it was like a poke to his heart. The constant reminder was a burr under his saddle rubbing a raw spot.

He took a deep breath. "I'll make you another one."

"Okay. In a pot of water on the stove. That way it won't be black. Grace said so."

He did as requested and managed to get the fries out of the oven without burning *them*. Having the eat-a-vegetable "discussion" wasn't high on his list right now, so applesauce would have to do.

Cassie made a face when he started to put ketchup on her plate. "Grace lets me do it by myself."

He handed her the plastic bottle and didn't say a word when she squeezed out enough for the whole town to dig in.

Cassie ate her fries first, delicately dipping them in the mountain of red sauce on her plate. Then she took a bite of her hot dog and said with her mouth full, "Do you think Grace misses me?"

"I'm sure she does." Why did he feel responsible for Cassie being sad? Grace was always temporary. "Kiddo, you do know that Grace was never going to stay here, right?"

"Yes." She looked at him solemnly. "But I hoped you'd ask her to."

He had asked. It didn't go well. That wasn't quite true. Things were perfect, until his father came and messed with his head. But he wondered why Cassie would even think he'd ask Grace not to go. She was only five. Was it just being a girl? Female intuition? Because he knew for a fact she had never seen him kiss Grace. Or even touch her for that matter.

"Why did you think I might ask Grace to stay?"

"Because you like her. And she likes you. A lot," she added emphatically.

"Did she say that?" Now who was hoping?

"No. I could just tell you liked her."

"Of course I do. She was here to take care of you."

"That's not it. You *like* her."

"Didn't I just say that?" he asked.

"No." A thoughtful look scrunched up her face. "You like her the way Mommy likes Denver."

The kid was talking love. He wasn't going to debate that, but he couldn't resist asking. "Why do you say that?"

She shrugged her small shoulders. "You were happy when Grace was here. Now you're not. Your eyes are kind of sad."

Was he that obvious? Apparently so if a five-year-old noticed. He'd thought having Cassie for the weekend would push away the loneliness. It always had before, but not now. Not since Grace.

He had to believe that letting her go was the right thing to do. For her sake.

It had been less than a week since Grace left Logan and Blackwater Lake in her rearview mirror, and that time had made no difference in how much his rejection still hurt. The fact that she even thought such a thing gave her a bad feeling that she would never get over him.

"You've beaten those eggs within an inch of their lives, Gracie. Is it those poor, innocent yolks you're mad at? Or something else?"

She looked down at the frothy, pulverized yellow stuff in the bowl, then her landlady. Janice Erwin was in her sixties, wore her silver hair in a sassy pixie cut and had the warmest brown eyes ever. The two of them were making breakfast together in the cozy country kitchen of the house where she rented a room. Jan stood beside her, in front of the deep sink. She was washing strawberries while Grace handled, or mishandled, the eggs.

"I was just daydreaming." About Logan. But she kept that part to herself.

Memories of the handsome rancher seemed woven into the fabric of her soul. That wasn't poetic, just a fact. And depressing because it meant that, unlike Lance the Loser, she would never get over the cowboy she'd left behind.

"You've been daydreaming a lot since you came back from that job in Blackwater Lake." Jan's eyes had gone from warm to questioning and concerned.

Grace wasn't sure how to answer and simply said, "Have I?"

"Yes, you have." Her landlady turned off the water. "Come to think of it, you haven't said much about work there. What did you think of the town?"

"Have you ever been there?" Grace was stalling. She wanted time to form a detached response.

"Never had the chance to myself. Andy worked at one of the ranches when he was younger."

Jan was a widow. Her daughters were grown and living with their families in California. After Andy died, she sold the ranch and downsized to this house with its white siding, green-painted shutters, wood floors and lots of room in the backyard for her garden and flowers.

When Grace invested her savings in a house that would never be hers, owned by a man who never cared about her, Jan offered her a place to stay and wouldn't take no for an answer. Friends helped friends, she'd said. To make sure they stayed friends, Grace insisted on paying rent. Jan had said she could use the extra money, but Grace always suspected the woman was lonely, too.

"What did your husband think of Blackwater Lake?"

"He wanted to stay. Said it was beautiful country with the lake and mountains. Nice people, too. Then we met, fell in love and decided to buy a piece of land and raise our girls here in Buckskin Pass." Jan dried her hands on a dish towel. "Is it still like that?"

"One of the prettiest places I've ever seen." Not that Grace had seen many places. But the lush trees, towering peaks and crystal-clear water had spoken to her soul. Darn it. There was that stupid poetic streak again. Love didn't just crush her heart; it was making her feel like a fool, too.

"Good to know Blackwater Lake hasn't changed. Wish I could say it hadn't changed you."

It took several moments for the words to sink in because Grace was still hung up on the downside of love. "You think I'm different?"

"No question about it, sweetie."

So it showed that something happened to her. And she thought she'd been hiding it awfully well. "I don't know what to say."

"It might be good to start with what went on while you were there," Jan suggested.

"I just did my job. Taking care of Cassie."

"The five-year-old?"

"Yes." An image of the adorable little girl who had tea parties and loved riding a horse popped into Grace's mind. The memory was swiftly followed by an empty feeling in the pit of her stomach. "Taking care of that little munchkin didn't feel like work."

"And you miss her."

"Yeah." Grace hoped that was enough of an explanation. What happened between her and Logan was something she wanted to forget as fast as possible.

There was a puzzled expression on Jan's softly lined face. "Is Cassie the only one you miss?"

There was a twinge in her chest, right in the area around her heart. "She's the one I spent most of my time with."

"That's not what I asked," the older woman said gently. "Tell me about Cassie's father."

"Logan."

"So that's his name."

"Yes. Logan Hunt." Who was really a Hart in spite of changing his name.

"And?"

"What? He hired me to take care of his daughter until her mom got home from an extended honeymoon. He paid me enough so that I now have the money for a down payment on my own house."

Grace had been so sure that buying a home and putting down roots would fix everything, but now she wasn't so sure. Instead of excitement at the prospect of having what she'd always wanted, she only felt let down and emptier than she ever had before.

"Hmm." Jan picked up the colander filled with washed strawberries and tilted it from side to side, draining the excess water.

"What does that mean?"

"Nothing. I just thought you would look happier about being able to go house hunting."

That's because she didn't need to hunt. She'd already found the place for her, and it was on Logan's ranch in

Blackwater Lake. When he'd asked her to leave, the door to her dream slammed shut in her face. There was no recovering from that.

"I am happy about it," she lied.

Jan smiled at her, but it didn't completely erase her concern. "I've never once regretted having you here in my home, Grace. In fact, I feel as if you're my third daughter."

Grace's throat closed with emotion for several moments. Kindness like that could pry the tears out of her, the ones she'd been holding back since leaving Logan. When she could form words without her voice breaking, she said, "And you feel like the mother I never had."

"Oh, sweetie—" The older woman pressed her lips together for a moment, controlling her own emotions. "I'm so going to miss you when you're gone."

"I'm not moving to Mars. We'll have lunch and run into each other at the grocery store and in town." And it occurred to her how difficult living in Blackwater Lake would have been, the chance of running into Logan always hanging over her. It would crush her all over again every time she saw him.

"It won't be the same," Jan said, smiling sadly.

"You're going to make me cry." Grace sniffled.

The other woman studied her. "The tears are there in you, but I'm not the only one responsible. Tell me what happened with you and that little girl's father. You'll feel better if you talk about it."

"Nothing will make me feel better, I'm afraid. And you have no idea how much I really don't want to talk about this." Grace sucked in a shuddering breath. "But you are more than just my friend, and you deserve more than an evasive answer."

"Come on, honey, this sounds like a kitchen table talk."

She let the older woman lead her to the round oak table

with its green cloth place mats and tin pitcher filled with pink, purple and yellow wildflowers. They sat in the ladder-back chairs and faced each other, knees nearly touching.

"Okay," Jan said. "Tell me what's wrong."

"I slept with Logan." Grace's eyes widened, and she slapped a hand over her mouth. That was not the way she'd planned to start this conversation. "Oh—wow—you must think I'm a horrible person."

"I'm old, honey, but not so ancient that I don't remember wanting to have sex with a man more than anything else in the whole world."

"Still—I was there for child care not...*that*." Her cheeks felt hot. "He was the strong, noble one. I pushed him into it. Don't judge."

"Good gravy, that's the last thing I'd do," Jan assured her. "Actually, I'm lying about that. My judgment is that you're one of the best and strongest women I've ever met. Against the odds, what with being abandoned by your mother, you've turned into a sweet, beautiful, honorable, principled person."

"That means a lot to me coming from you."

"Now that that's out of the way… Tell me about this Logan."

"He's a good man. Such a good father, although he doesn't see that. He's overprotective in the best possible way. Just trying his darnedest to always do the right thing. Especially for his daughter."

"Then what's the problem?"

"His father was not a very good husband, and his family fell apart. Logan is afraid he's like that and he'll destroy any woman he cares about."

"So he won't let himself care," Jan concluded.

"Yes." Tears filled Grace's eyes. "Unfortunately, I care about him quite a lot."

She explained the rest, everything from Logan wanting her to stay, then his father showing up to push for a relationship with his granddaughter. And finally Logan asking her to leave.

"I think he feels something."

Jan nodded her agreement. "He would have let you go when your contract was up if he didn't."

"I was a kid no one wanted, and it's easy to see when someone has a lot of love to give. Logan does, but he just can't bring himself to give it to me—"

Grace lost it then and started to cry. She covered her face with her hands as sobs tore through her. Then she felt Jan's arms come around her.

"Oh, sweetie, I'm so sorry you're hurting." The older woman's tone was sympathetic and angry at the same time. "If you ask me, the man is a jackass."

"I know." Grace dropped her hands and gave the woman a wobbly smile. "But he's the jackass I love."

Chapter Fifteen

On Sunday around dinnertime, Logan stopped his truck in front of the pretty two-story house with the oval etched-glass front door and the flower-lined brick path. "Home, sweet home, baby girl."

"I'm not a baby, Daddy. I've told you and told you." She gave him the long-suffering look that said he was dumb as dirt.

"You'll always be my baby and I'll be calling you that even when you're twenty-five."

"Wow, that's so *old*."

Which would make him ancient. Lately he'd felt that way more than he ever had before. Missing Grace took the color out of everything. But he managed to smile at his daughter and did his best to savor the moment. Because after handing her off to her mother, he would be going back to the ranch that was too quiet, too bare.

He tried to keep Grace out of his head, but she refused to stay away. That would take time. But even as he thought it, doubts crept in. A million years wouldn't be long enough to forget her.

He opened the driver's door. "Let's go see your mom."

"Okay, Daddy."

On the passenger side he helped her down, then retrieved her small pink princess suitcase from the rear seat. Logan rested his hand on her shoulder as they walked up the path to the front door. Cassie rang the doorbell, and moments later an indistinct figure appeared in the glass just as the dead bolt turned.

The door opened and Tracy smiled. "Hi, you guys."

Cassie went in and hugged her. "Hi, Mommy."

"Now, that's a good hug, Cass. Your hugs have been super hard since I got home. Either you got really big and strong while I was on my honeymoon or you missed me a lot while I was away."

"It sure was long." The pouty little look was designed to produce the maximum amount of guilt.

Logan wondered if she practiced that expression in front of the mirror. It was perfect and worked like a charm on him.

"How long are you going to hold it against me that I went away?" Tracy took the pout in stride and smiled. "I've been back a week now. And I dare you to tell me you didn't have fun while I was gone. After all, your dad let you ride a horse."

Cassie snapped out of her little snit and grinned. "I did have fun."

"I thought so. Now, go wash up for dinner."

"Can Daddy stay?"

"Sure." She met his gaze. "Would you like to?"

"I don't want to intrude." He set Cassie's suitcase just inside the door. "You're a married woman now."

Tracy made a dismissive sound and closed the door. "If it was a problem, I would tell you. And you know that. We've been friends too long to play games."

"Yeah." He was grateful for her friendship. "I just wanted to make sure your husband doesn't mind."

"Den?" Tracy waved her hand. "He wouldn't care even if he was going to be here. He's at the office. Figured Cassie was with you and we didn't have plans so he'd put in a couple hours of work. He's still catching up on stuff that accumulated while we were gone. Being a busy accountant is a good thing, but his partner couldn't keep up with everything."

"You're sure you don't mind?" He shouldn't question her too hard because dinner here meant he could put off facing that empty house.

"I'd like the company." Tracy's gaze narrowed on him. "You didn't even ask what I'm making. That's not like you. What if the menu is quiche and brussels sprouts?"

To be honest, he didn't care if it was bread and water. For just a little while he would be distracted from wanting Grace so badly he ached in places he'd never known were there.

"I hate quiche and brussels sprouts." He shuddered.

"Like I said. Friends for a long time. We're having pot roast and mashed potatoes."

"My favorite."

"Den's, too. Plus it will be good left over when he can see his way clear to abandoning numbers and spreadsheets and come home to his loving and devoted wife." She looked down at her daughter. "I believe you were asked to wash up for dinner."

"I was hopin' you forgot," Cassie said.

"Not a chance. You've been in Daddy's barn and riding horses." She wrinkled her nose at the thought. "Who knows what you touched. Now scoot."

"Ookay." Cassie sighed, then dragged herself down the hall to the bathroom.

"And you can set the table," Tracy told him.

He washed his hands at the kitchen sink, then did as requested. This was Tracy's house, and he knew where everything was. But there were signs that a man lived here now. Athletic shoes by the back door. A flannel shirt hung on a hook beside it. Her husband's baseball hat hanging on the shirt.

"So," he said. "Den moved in here."

"Temporarily." Tracy stirred gravy in a pot on the stove.

"Trouble in paradise?"

"What?" She looked up, then laughed. "No. I meant that we're going to look for a house together. Eventually. We didn't want Cassie to experience a lot of changes all at once. New house. Starting kindergarten. A man sleeping in Mommy's bed."

Logan thought she looked happier than he'd ever seen her. The glow was probably visible from space. Envy knifed through him, not that he begrudged her having it all. Just that he didn't have anything close.

"I take it you have no regrets about tying the knot."

Her smile was radiant. "No."

"Well, marriage looks good on you." He nodded. "You guys make a great couple."

"Speaking of couples…" Tracy turned the burner down to low and met his gaze.

It suddenly felt as if she'd turned the heat *up* on him. "Whatever you're going to say—don't."

"Have you been in touch with Grace since she left?"

"What part of 'don't ask' did you not understand?"

"Seriously?" She put her hands on her hips. "This is me. Your best friend. And I want to know about you and Grace."

"There is no me and Grace." Although he had to admit there was a nice ring to linking their names. But he'd blown any possible chance of that happening.

"Why not?"

Logan was instantly on the defensive. "I don't understand the question."

"Oh, brother." She shook her head. "You're not really that dense, are you?"

"There's no good answer to that, so I'm not even going to try."

"Then just listen." Tracy's look was sympathetic. "There was a spark between you and Grace. I saw the way she looked at you. And, believe me, I've never seen you look at any woman the way you did her. I expected flames any second."

The knot in his gut twisted tighter as the truth of her words sank in. But admitting she was right would make his pushing her away even more real. "You haven't seen every woman I've ever looked at."

"Maybe not. But I've seen enough, and I know you." She sighed. "She stayed on after her contract was up. Everyone in Blackwater Lake knows, so don't give me that look. Obviously you asked her to hang around. I'm only surprised you let her go at all."

"I didn't actually *let* her go." Logan rubbed a hand over the back of his neck. "It was best for her."

"You threw her out?" Tracy's voice was pitched quite a bit higher.

"Not exactly." Liar. That's exactly what he'd done. "The thing is, I didn't want to hurt her."

"Oh, Logan—I'd so hoped Grace had gotten through to you, convinced you that you're not a heartless man."

Like his father. But Grace was the first one to make him question the bitterness he'd carried around all these years. "She got me thinking."

"Good." Tracy's approval didn't last long. "And then you shot yourself in the foot? Cut off your nose to spite your face? Threw the baby out with the bathwater—"

"I get it."

"Do you?" Her eyes flashed. "If you did, you would have moved heaven and earth to keep her here."

"Her life is in Buckskin Pass."

"People relocate all the time for reasons less important than love." She stared him down. "Tell me you're not in love with Grace."

He wanted to. He wished he wasn't. But confirming it would never happen. Somehow he knew saying those words out loud would rip his heart to shreds.

"It's my fault she left. And before you say anything, you're right. I'm an idiot." He glared at her. "Are you happy now?"

There was only pity in her eyes. "I'm so sorry, Logan. It's just that you and Grace were so good together."

Cassie came running into the kitchen, and there was no way she hadn't heard what her mother said. "I miss Grace. Daddy, are you going to marry her?"

"Honey, I—"

"You have to," she said. "She can be Belle and you're Prince Adam."

Beauty and the Beast. Was it life imitating art? Could he really have the family he'd always wanted?

Logan went down on one knee in front of his daughter. "I can't make any promises, baby girl."

But he had to try to fix things.

After looking at houses with her real estate agent, Grace still wasn't as excited as she'd expected to be. She'd seen a cute little cottage that was perfect for her and planned to give herself twenty-four hours to think it over before making her final decision. A place of her own had been her goal for as long as she could remember, and she was so close to reaching it. Instead of jumping up and down, she wanted to pull the bedcovers over her head.

"This is all Logan's fault," she muttered to herself.

But that wasn't fair. He'd warned her not to fall for him, although that was like telling her not to breathe. It was just that loving him when he couldn't love her back had sucked all the joy right out of her dream.

She was headed back to her rented room at Jan's house and turned left onto Saddleback Street. As she drove closer, she noticed there was a truck parked at the curb. A very familiar red truck, the very one that Logan had picked her up and put her in on the day of Tracy's wedding. The memory of being in his arms backhanded her heart in an especially painful way.

Why was he here? Did she leave something at the ranch? If she had, he could have mailed it. So why drive all this way from Blackwater Lake? Her heart was pounding by the time she pulled her car into the driveway behind Jan's. It took every ounce of determination she had not to back right out and burn rubber to get out of there.

Hope was the cruelest emotion ever. All her life, every move from one placement to the next, she hoped this was when a family would want her and she'd have a place to belong. That never happened, and hope turned into her worst nightmare. But right this second she knew every one of those letdowns was nothing compared with how Logan could destroy her if she let herself hope this time.

Grace got out of the car and walked up the three steps, then opened the front door. In Jan's living room there were two floral-print love seats facing each other. Her landlady was sitting on one with a cup of tea on the oak coffee table in front of her. Logan sat on the other, his back to the door, but he stood and looked at her when she came inside and closed it.

"Look who's here, Grace." Jan smiled and her tone was friendly, but her eyes told a different story. She was definitely Team Grace. "Logan and I have been getting acquainted while you were house hunting."

He held his Stetson in his hands. "Hi, Grace. How are you?"

"Fine, thanks." It was on the tip of her tongue to ask what he was doing so far from home. But after what happened the last time they were together, she was in no mood to make this easy on him. She deliberately let the silence drag on.

Finally, he cleared his throat. "Did you find a house?"

"Yes." He had no right to the information that she was mulling it over.

"Oh."

"That's great, Gracie." Jan picked up her cup and took a sip of tea then replaced it on the saucer. "Where is it?"

"The Matthews place on Cheyenne Court."

"I know it." The landlady nodded her approval. "That's closer to the elementary school for work and looks really nice from the outside."

"The interior needs a little cosmetic attention, but I can take my time with that."

"Congratulations," Logan said. "So you put a down payment on it?"

"My agent advised me to give it twenty-four hours to see if it still feels right. So I'll be doing that tomorrow."

A spark of something popped in his eyes. "Would it be all right if I talked to you? Right now?"

"Of course." She folded her arms over her chest.

He hesitated for a moment and looked at Jan. "Alone?"

Her friend started to get up, but Grace put up a hand. "Stay right where you are."

"Okay." Jan sat back down.

"So, what's on your mind, Logan?"

He tossed the Stetson onto the love seat and met her gaze. "I'm sorry for what I did to you. I wasn't prepared when my father showed up. It threw me. I took it out on you, and that was wrong. You deserve so much better."

"I could not agree with you more." Grace held her head high. "So, I accept your apology, and if that's all—"

"It's not." He glanced at Jan for just a moment, then back to her. "Cassie misses you."

Double whammy to her heart, and she took a moment before saying anything. "I miss her, too."

"She's not the only one."

"Oh?" Darn it. Hope didn't seem inclined to behave itself and started to stir inside her.

He continued as if she was the only person in the room. "I miss you, Grace. More than I can say. Nothing is the same without you."

Grace did her level best to keep hope at bay, but between the sincerity in his eyes and the words she'd longed to hear it was pretty much impossible. Still, she tried one more time. "I'm sorry to hear that, Logan. But I was only hired for a limited time."

"That's not what I'm talking about, and you know it. This thing between us has nothing to do with your contract." He looked down for a few seconds and blew out a breath. "I didn't want to. I tried to stop and couldn't. The thing is, I fell in love with you, Grace."

"Oh, my—that is my cue to leave you two alone." Jan sniffled, then stood and walked over to Grace.

"Please don't leave me," she begged.

"Oh, honey. You got this." The other woman leaned in close and whispered, "Just my opinion and worth what you paid for it, but I'm thinking he's not really a jackass."

Grace watched her friend leave, then looked at Logan. "I don't know why I should believe you."

His gaze never left hers. "You were right. About everything. I'm not my father, and the truth is, he's not all bad."

"What made you change your mind about that?"

"You." He took a step closer, and their bodies were

inches apart. "Because of you I began to question what happened. My conclusions and everything I believed about him and myself."

"And?" Although she wanted to throw herself into his arms, she needed to hear the words as much as he needed to say them.

"My father is a flawed man. I talked to my brothers and sister, and all of us agree on that. But you had a point when you said there's a little bit of right on the other side of wrong. He's guilty of being selfish and unfaithful, but it wasn't his intention to abandon his children." He told her what Tucker had said about their grandfather running him off the ranch. "I've been stupid and I was afraid of being like him—or what I thought he was."

"Now you're not?"

"No comment on the stupid part." His mouth curved up for a moment, a ghost of a smile. "But I'm not afraid anymore. I would never hurt someone I love. But I am scared of losing you. I barely made it through a week after you left. No way I can go the rest of my life without you. I love you, Grace."

Just when she'd thought her dream would never happen, in walked this show-don't-tell cowboy with the words that put her heart back together. "Was that so hard?"

"Falling in love with you was the easiest thing in the world. The hard part was letting go of the past." Logan gave her a smile that made her want to take her clothes off. Then he went down on one knee and took her hands in his. "I know buying a house of your own is what you always wanted. But if you would do me the honor of becoming my wife, I promise I will make it up to you."

She'd dreamed of belonging but always pictured a place, not a person. Being this happy was not something she had ever let herself believe in but here it was. And he was waiting for her answer. "A house is just a building. Wherever you and Cassie are is home. I love you, too. So, yes, I'll marry you."

Logan closed his eyes for a moment, then nodded, as if he'd had grave doubts about her answer. He stood and pulled her against him, sealing their promise with a kiss. More than once growing up she'd wished for a family like all the other kids had. But the pain and loneliness of her childhood had brought her to this place, this time, in the arms of the man she loved more than anything. *Worth it*, she thought happily.

Epilogue

Three months later

It was his wedding day and Logan was surprisingly calm. He would have married Grace that day in Buckskin Pass right after he proposed, but she insisted on waiting. School was starting soon, and she wouldn't leave the kids in the lurch for a kindergarten teacher. Fortunately, the school board quickly found a replacement for her, and after officially resigning, she moved to the ranch.

Most important, they needed to tell Cassie. Logan had no reservations. After all, his daughter was the one who'd asked if he was going to marry Grace, but she insisted on being sure his little girl was secure and happy about the whole thing. She was—especially the part where she got to be a flower girl again.

Today, she would be. In the house that had been in his family for generations, he was going to marry the love of his life. But first there was something he had to do. A promise he had to keep before he swore to love her forever. He knocked on the bedroom door where his bride-to-be was getting ready for the ceremony.

"Who is it?" That was Jamie's voice. His sister was the maid of honor.

"Is she decent?" he asked.

"Have I ever been?" The joy in Grace's voice made him smile.

"I need to talk to you," he said.

"Daddy, you can't see the bride before the wedding. It's bad luck."

Impossible, he thought. Since the moment Grace had walked into this house, fate or karma or whatever you wanted to call it had been nothing but on his side. This woman had given him his life.

"I have to talk to Grace," he repeated firmly. "I'll close my eyes."

"You're not going to back down on this, are you?" Jamie asked.

"No. Not unless Grace has a problem with it."

Her voice came from just on the other side of the door. "This is really that important to you?"

"Yes."

"Okay, then."

"I want to go on record as being against this." The door opened and Jamie was standing there in a red dress with a long flowing skirt and lace sleeves from shoulder to wrist.

"Big difference from your scrubs," he said. "You don't look half bad, sis."

She smiled and straightened his black bow tie that went with the traditional black tuxedo. "You're not so bad yourself. Just so you know, I take my maid of honor duties seriously. I advised Grace to run while there was still time, but she refused."

"She's kidding," Grace said from behind the door.

"How do I look, Daddy, in my flower girl dress?" Cassie twirled around, and the red velvet skirt billowed around her.

There was a lump of emotion in his throat as he stared at his beautiful child. "You take my breath away."

"Is that good?"

"Very." He looked down at her. "Are you all ready?"

She nodded. "I can't wait. Now I'll have a mom at both of my houses."

"That makes me so happy—" Grace's voice broke.

"Come with Aunt Jamie, Cass. If this goes on much longer the bride will have to redo her makeup. Hurry it up," she ordered him.

"Okay."

"Close your eyes," his daughter ordered him.

"Will do." He did as requested and heard his sister take Cassie out in the hall to wait by the top of the stairs. In a few minutes the action would start, and he could hardly wait to make Grace his.

He closed the door behind him and opened his eyes. "Sorry."

"It's all right. The bad-luck thing is an urban myth." Grace smiled up at him.

And then he really looked at her and was afraid he'd swallowed his tongue. The bodice of her dress was white lace over satin, and the skirt was full, flowing and feminine. The delicate veil was secured with flowers at the knot of curls on top of her head.

Logan literally could not breathe for several moments. "Wow."

"That's the best you've got?"

"Sorry. There are no words that would do justice to how beautiful you are."

"Don't you make me cry, too." Her eyes glistened as she smiled happily. "So, what can't wait until after we're married?"

"Oh, right. I have your wedding gift." He pulled some papers from the inside pocket of his black jacket. "My lawyer drew these up. It puts your name on the ranch title. This land and house officially belong to both of us."

"What?"

"When you gave up buying a house, I promised to make it up to you. Now I have. It's important you know that before we get married."

She looked at the paper, then him. The tears in her eyes slipped down her cheeks. "Logan—"

"You have a home, Grace. It's official. A place to put down roots. A place to belong. With me. And I belong with you."

"I'm doing my very best not to sob. That wouldn't be a good look for the pictures." She pressed her lips together, then blew out a breath. "I don't know what to say."

"You don't have long to get over that because in a couple of minutes we're going to promise to love, honor and respect each other forever."

"It's really only two words." She threw her arms around his neck. "I do."

"I do, too."

Logan kissed her gently, then left to take his place beside the minister in front of their guests. After Grace descended the stairs and put her hand in his, they repeated those private I dos in front of friends and family, including his father. With cheers and applause erupting around them, Logan kissed his wife.

"I love you, Mrs. Hunt," he said. "My Grace."

And she was just what the cowboy needed.

* * * * *

If you loved this book, be sure to check out
Teresa Southwick's next book, part of the next
MONTANA MAVERICKS *continuity,*
coming out in October 2018!

And until then, catch up with all of
THE BACHELORS OF BLACKWATER LAKE:

THE NEW GUY IN TOWN
JUST A LITTLE BIT MARRIED
A WORD WITH THE BACHELOR
HOW TO LAND HER LAWMAN

Available now wherever Harlequin Special Edition
books and ebooks are sold!

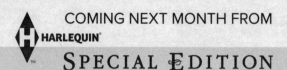

COMING NEXT MONTH FROM
HARLEQUIN®
SPECIAL EDITION

Available January 16, 2018

#2599 NO ORDINARY FORTUNE
The Fortunes of Texas: The Rulebreakers • by Judy Duarte
Carlo Mendoza always thought he had the market cornered on charm, until he met Schuyler Fortunado. She's a force of nature—and secretly a Fortune! And when Schuyler takes a job with Carlo at the Mendoza Winery, sparks fly!

#2600 A SOLDIER IN CONARD COUNTY
American Heroes • by Rachel Lee
After an injury places him on indefinite leave, Special Forces sergeant Gil York ends up in Conard County to escape his overbearing family. Miriam Baker, a gentle music teacher, senses Gil needs more than a place to stay and coaxes him out from behind his walls. But is he willing to face his past to make a future with Miriam?

#2601 AN ENGAGEMENT FOR TWO
Matchmaking Mamas • by Marie Ferrarella
The Matchmaking Mamas are at it again, this time for Mikki McKenna, a driven internist who has always shied away from commitment. But when Jeff Sabatino invites her to dine at his restaurant and sparks a chance at a relationship, she begins to wonder if this table for two might be worth the risk after all.

#2602 A BRIDE FOR LIAM BRAND
The Brands of Montana • by Joanna Sims
Kate King has settled into her role as rancher and mother, but with her daughter exploring her independence, she thinks she might want to give handsome Liam Brand a chance. But her ex and his daughter are both determined to cause trouble, and Kate and Liam will have to readjust their visions of the future to claim their own happily-ever-after.

#2603 THE SINGLE DAD'S FAMILY RECIPE
The McKinnels of Jewell Rock • by Rachael Johns
Single-dad chef Lachlan McKinnell is opening a restaurant at his family's whiskey distillery and struggling to find a suitable head hostess. Trying to recover from tragedy, Eliza Coleman thinks a move to Jewell Rock and a job at a brand-new restaurant could be the fresh start she's looking for. She never expected to fall for her boss, but it's beginning to look like they have all the ingredients for a perfect family!

#2604 THE MARINE'S SECRET DAUGHTER
Small-Town Sweethearts • by Carrie Nichols
When he returns to his hometown, marine Riley Cooper finds the girl he left behind living next door. But there's more between them than the heartbreak they gave each other—and five-year-old Fiona throws quite a wrench in their reunion. Will Riley choose the marines and a safe heart, or will he risk it all on the family he didn't even know he had?

Get 2 Free Books,
Plus 2 Free Gifts—
just for trying the Reader Service!

SPECIAL EXCERPT FROM

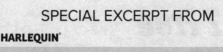

HARLEQUIN®

SPECIAL EDITION

Special Forces sergeant Gil York ends up in Conard County to escape his overbearing family, only to run into Miriam Baker, a gentle music teacher who tries to coax him out from behind the walls he's constructed around his heart and soul.

Read on for a sneak preview of the second **AMERICAN HEROES** *story,* A SOLDIER IN CONARD COUNTY, *by* New York Times *bestselling author* Rachel Lee.

"Sorry," she said. "I just feel so helpless. Talk away. I'll keep my mouth shut."

"I don't want that." Then he caused her to catch her breath by sliding down the couch until he was right beside her. He slipped his arm around her shoulders, and despite her surprise, it seemed the most natural thing in the world to lean into him and finally let her head come to rest on his shoulder.

"Holding you is nice," he said quietly. "You quiet the rat race in my head. Does that sound awful?"

How could it? she wondered, when she'd been amazed at the way he had caused her to melt, as if everything else went away and she was in a warm, soft, safe space. If she could offer him any part of that, she would, gladly.

"If that sounds like I'm using you…"

"Man, don't you ever stop? Do you ever just go with the flow?" Turning and tilting her head a bit, she pressed a quick kiss on his lips.

"What the…" He sounded surprised.

"You're analyzing constantly," she told him. "This isn't a mission. Let it go. Let go. Just relax and hold me, and I hope you're enjoying it as much as I am."

Because she was. That wonderful melting filled her again, leaving her soft and very, very content. Maybe even happy.

"You are?" he murmured.

"I am. More than I've ever enjoyed a hug." God, had she ever been this blunt with a man before? But this guy was so bound up behind his walls and drawbridges, she wondered if she'd need a sledgehammer to get through.

But then she remembered Al and the distance she'd sensed in him during his visits. Not exactly alone, but alone among family. These guys had been deeply changed by their training and experience. Where did they find comfort now? Real comfort?

Her thoughts were slipping away in response to a growing anticipation and anxiety. She was close, so close to him, and his strength drew her like a bee to nectar. He even smelled good, still carrying the scents from the storm outside and his earlier shower, but beneath that the aroma of male.

Everything inside her became focused on one trembling hope, that he'd take this hug further, that he'd draw her closer and begin to explore her with his hands and mouth.

Don't miss
A SOLDIER IN CONARD COUNTY by Rachel Lee,
available February 2018 wherever
Harlequin® Special Edition books and ebooks are sold.

www.Harlequin.com

Looking for more satisfying love stories
with community and family at their core?

Check out **Harlequin® Special Edition**
and **Harlequin® Western Romance** books!

New books available every month!

CONNECT WITH US AT:

Harlequin.com/Community

ReaderService.com

**ROMANCE WHEN
YOU NEED IT**

HFGENRE2017R